# TENEMENT ECHOES

# THE BACK STORY

Many small New England cities became magnets for immigrants from Italy Lebanon France Poland Germany and other countries because textile manufacturing companies were offering jobs providing a minimal but adequate and livable wage. Many of these immigrant's families lived in cold water tenement houses heated by a fuel burning stove in the kitchen. They were very simply furnished with sofas and beds covered with handmade quilts. The floors were covered with linoleum and the kitchen table covered with a few yards of colorful oil cloth and the windows adorned with plastic draperies. But those living conditions were far superior to what these people had left in their home countries. The second world war imposed other hardships with many first-generation young men being drafted and too many of them returning wounded physically and or mentally and some not returning at all. Those heart aches greatly diluted or eliminated the marginal happiness many of these families were experiencing. Two cereal box tops and a quarter (if you could do enough errands to earn a quarter) could be sent away for a magic ring which would glow in the dark allow you to send signals and it had a hidden compartment. Penny candy choices we're many but pennies weren't. Telephones were a luxury. People in the tenants would signal the other neighbors by a series of pre-determined taps on the cold-water pipe that deliver water to the kitchen sinks in each tenement. The main source of entertainment was the fifteen-cent movie and the and a nickel bought you a candy bar or bag of popcorn. There were no televisions, so the radio provided several family orientated serial programs. Patched trousers, darned socks, hand woven gloves, scarves and hats, and cotton house dresses…all those were about as *haute* as the *couture* except for the hand me down Sunday suits for the boys and the handmade special occasion dresses for the girls. That was their material world; however, their emotional world was not unlike that of any family regardless of wealth and status because love, laughter, tears, and pain are experienced the same whether you are wearing a tattered cotton hat or diamond tiara. During the war the most iconic harbinger of fear and loss was the Western Union man because he inevitably brought the *missing in action* or *wounded in action* telegrams to the families.

Because of language and cultural barriers ethnic communities socialized among themselves and the lifestyles and each of the tenements was so similar that going from one to another was seamless. There was always a pot of coffee brewing and on the table, there was always a dish of olives, some cheese or yogurt and a loaf of the daily baked bread. There were nightly card games followed by grilled cheese sandwiches and stories about the old country These are all *tenement echoes.*

TIME: 1944—1945.

PLACE: Poor working neighborhood in a New England mill town

CHARACTERS; In order of appearance

> NELLIE: Early 30's, trim, brunette, potentially very attractive...simple cotton housedresses, no makeup, hair. . .very simply styled.

JOEY: Adolescent, thin, energetic but frail looking, usually wearing knickers and knee socks, cap and high-top shoes.

. RICHIE; Same age as Joey, shorter, heavier, Mediterranean features, dresses in the same manner as Joey.

ARLENE: also, adolescent, medium height, slender…wears baggy clothes, no makeup, hair simply combed and always nervously agitated.

MARCIA: Same physique as Arline but wears clothes that accentuate her great figure, and her hair style and makeup are .pronounced

WESTERN UNION MAN: A short, thin, late 50's.

BENJY: A medium built man in his 50's, with slicked back hair, wears a *zoot suit*, open shirt, loosely knotted tie, and keeps a cigar in the corner of his mouth.

BELLA: A stocky woman, also late 50's, with very closely cropped hair…masculine in appearance and actions.

Mrs. COURY: Similar to Bella in appearance...she wears a plain cloth coat and a cloth hat, thick beige stockings, and heavy heeled, black, laced shoes.

ANNIE: Mid 60s, looking every bit her age, short and frail (Helen Hayes or Jessica Tandy type), always in a cotton housedress, never any makeup, grey hair pulled back in a bun.

TOMMY: Mid 20 's, medium height, slender, good looking athlete.

TED: Early 30 s, ruggedly handsome, usually unshaven, dark hair.

FATHER ELIAR: Mid 40's, balding, paunchy, closet drinker .

SIMONE: Mid 30's, dark hair, sexy, seductive prostitute...exhibiting all the trademarks and scars of her profession... tough but savvy.

DELIA: Petite woman, early 60's desperately holding onto memories of youth in a tattered but exaggerated way...frilly dresses, cheap red curly wig, heavy pancake makeup, false eyelashes, bright rouge and lipstick and nail polish.

## ACT I

### SCENE I

SETTING: Nellie is in the tenement kitchen at the ironing board and in the bedroom, you can see Joey and Richie sitting in front of the radio, Joey intent on the program, Richie more intent on the girly. magazine he is thumbing through.

(You hear from off stage someone yell: *Mailman's here.*)

NELLIE

I hope it's not the Western Union man.

> (She quickly and anxiously looks up at the clock. She blesses herself, clenches her hands tightly together, closes her eyes, says a brief prayer and blesses herself again.)

(In the bedroom Joey stands up and looks at Richie.)

JOEY

Come on! That's the mailman! Maybe he brought the ring!!

RICHIE

(Not raising his eyes from the magazine)

Yeah...That's great. why don't you go down and see while I finish looking through this new magazine?

JOEY

All you ever think about is sex. I bet you can't even remember one time when you didn't have sex on your mind!

RICHIE

Of course, I can! Let me see now? Hmm. . .
How about the time I fell off my bicycle on the
playground?

JOEY

That's because you had a concussion. . .you
were unconscious!

RICHIE

Yeah, well, that counts, doesn't it? When I
woke up, I do remember seeing that beautiful
nurse ᵗs boobs hanging over me. . . I almost
passed out again.

JOEY

You ᴵre hopeless. Are you going to come down
with me or not? I can't wait any longer.

RICHIE

All right. But can I use this picture to keep my
place?

JOEY

Are you crazy? That's St. Jude!

RICHIE

Yeah? (looking at the picture) Even better…maybe my prayers will be answered. (he quickly grabs his crotch)

JOEY

Very funny. Very funny. Where the hell did you get those magazines from anyway?

RICHIE

My cousin Ernie brought them back with him from France.

JOEY

It must be inherited.

RICHIE

What must be inherited?

JOEY

Being oversexed.

RICHIE

Speaking of my cousin Ernie, I᾽m kind of worried about him.

            JOEY

Why?

            RICHIE

Well, when I went into his bedroom to borrow this magazine, I found another one sticking out from under his pillow.

            JOEY

So, what?

            RICHIE

Well, that one showed both boys and girls without clothes on.

            JOEY

You mean you think he's....

            RICHIE

Yeah, I think he's ambisextrous?

JOEY

Ambisextrous? There's no such word. You're confusing the word with ambidextrous which means he can use either hand.

RICHIE

He can? Wow! I never tried it with my left hand!

(pantomiming masturbation)

JOEY

Are you coming with me or not?

RICHIE

Yeah, yeah. Let's go.

(Richie folds the magazine with St. Jude's picture in it and puts it in his back pocket. They walk into the kitchen and see Nellie.)

JOEY

Hey mom. I 'm going to rundown and see if the ring came. Remember the ring, Mom?

NELLIE

How can I forget the ring, sweetheart? For the last two weeks you 've been running up and down those stairs every time you heard a noise that even sounded like mailman slamming the door.

JOEY

Yeah remember the time at Mrs. Kowalski 's downstairs when the top of her pressure cooker blew off and hit the stove pipe?

NELLIE

I remember all right. How could I forget? I understand she's still finding beans and pieces of kielbasa in some of the strangest places in her kitchen. Her canary died you know.

RICHIE

Yeah, I know Butchie told me his mother's canary got hit with one of those pieces of kielbasa. Butchie said that his old man told him that it was better that the canary should die from being hit with the kielbasa than eating it. At least the bird didn't suffer from the gas that the old man always gets from Mrs. Kowalski 's cooking. Butchie says sometimes his house sounds like an artillery firing range.

(They all start laughing and Joey goes ahead. As the boys are heading downstairs You could see the mailboxes on either side of the door. Joey goes into the top mailbox and pulls out a manila paper covered package.)


JOEY

It's here! Look! The Lone Ranger ring has arrived!

RICHIE

Great. Hurry. . Open it up!

(As Joey unwraps the package Richie imitates the theme from the "Lone Ranger" radio show.)

RICHIE

Tarunt… tarunt…tarunt…from out of the past comes the sound of hooves of horses. It's the Lone Ranger! Hi, ho, Silver!

> (As they are doing that, the Western Union man walks toward the front door. Joey has just opened the package and the sheet of instructions is in his hands. When the Western Union man steps into the front door they both look at him in a frightened way, and Joey drops the sheet of instructions. The Western Union man reads the names on the mail boxes and his finger stops at one)

JOEY

It's for Mrs. Coury again.

RICHIE

It's got to be about Jimmie this time.

(looking out he says to the Western Union man)

Here come's Arlene Coury.

(Just then Arlene walks into the doorway and sees the Western Union man and nervously asks)

ARLENE

What do you want?

WESTERN UNION MAN

I 've got a telegram for you.

ARLENE

I don't want to take it. I can't ... It's bad news, I know it is. Come back when my mother is home from work. I don't want to take anything till she gets here.

WESTERN UNION MAN

Miss, you must take it. I can't come back. Unfortunately, I 've got a lot of these things to deliver today.

JOEY

Arlene, maybe it's not bad news. Remember last week when Mrs. Losodi got the news they found Frankie. That he wasn't missing anymore? Remember that? That was a telegram, too.

ARLENE

I remember. Maybe he 's on his way home!

RICHIE

Yeah, that 'd be a nice surprise for your mother, wouldn't, Arlene?

ARLENE

It sure would. Okay, I 'll take it.

(She takes the telegram. The fellow from Western Union leaves as she 's opening the telegram.)

Oh, my God! Oh, no! Jimmie! Jimmie! He 's dead! He's been killed in action. My mother's going to go crazy when she finds out. She 'll be home from work in a little while. I don't want to be the one to tell her.

(She runs in the hallway.)

JOEY

It seems like every morning now we see that godamn guy on his bicycle and after he leaves we hear the women screaming from one tenement or another. Jesus, when Mrs. Corey gets home, it 's going to be terrible.

RICHIE

You 're telling me. This is the second time for her.

## JOEY

I 'm going to go upstairs and tell Mum. Come over after lunch?

RICHIE

Okay.

(As Joey goes in and Richie 's about to
leave, he looks down and sees the sheet of
instructions for the ring and he sits on the
stoop and starts to read it. Joey walks in
the hallway and sees Arlene coming down
the stairs.)

JOEY

Where are you going?

ARLENE

I can 't face my mother. It was bad enough when my
brother Johnny died. I 'm going across the street to my
cousin's. He'll have to tell her. I just can't do it, Joey.

(She's about to leave but they see Mrs.
Coury, coming home from work, carrying
her lunch bag and Arlene hides behind the
door and Joey runs up to his tenement.)

MRS. COURY

Hello, Richie.

RICHIE

Oh, God! I didn't want to be here when you heard about it.

MRS. COURY

(Immediately sensing that what she feared every day had happened.)

Hear about what? What are you talking about? Tell me!

(She reaches down and physically stands him up by pulling on his sweater and starts shaking him vigorously.)

RICHIE

It's about Jimmie. It's about Jimmie. He's dead! The Western Union man came. He's dead.

MRS. COURY

(Hysterical)

You 're lying! You 're lying! Why are you telling me this? Why are you such a bad boy? Why are you saying these things?

> (She slaps him, and he turns away and runs up the street. She closes the door without seeing Arlene hiding behind it and goes running up the stairs shouting)

MRS. COURY

Arlene, Arlene? Where are you? It's not true, is it? It's not true! That little bastard was lying. Your brother Jimmie is all right, isn't he? Please God, let my boy be all right.

> (She goes up the stairs. The front door closes, and Arlene is standing in the hallway.)

ARLENE

(crushing the telegram against her face)

Oh, Momma, Momma! God help us!

(and runs out of the apartment house).

## SCENE II

SETTING: The apartment lights up and Joey's grandmother, Annie, can be seen.

ANNIE

What's all that noise out there? Who 's doing all that screaming? Something bad has happened.

> (She goes to the faucet and knocks twice on the pipe, and the upstairs apartment lights up and Joey's mother, Nellie, hears the noise and is about to respond when Joey comes in. He comes over to her and puts his arms around her.)

JOEY

. (out of breath and coughing spasmodically) .

The Western Union man came and said that Jimmie Coury died.

NELLIE

Oh, my God!

(Annie hits the pipe again twice. )

NELLIE

That ' s Grandma. She must be so frightened. Let me signal that everything is all right.

(Joey releases Nellie and she goes to the sink and wraps three times.)

ANNIE

(after she hears the signal)

I don't believe it. I saw it in the cards this morning. Something is wrong. . . I know it!

(She knocks twice again.)

NELLIE

(knocks three times)

I fixed you a sandwich, sweetheart. I'm going down to see grandma.

JOEY

(coughing)

I 'm not hungry, Mum...I'll eat later.

NELLIE

You 've got to eat…you know what the doctor said.

JOEY

I 'll eat after I listen to my radio programs. I don't want to miss them. Henry Aldrich is on.

NELLIE

You and those damn programs! Why do you like that Henry Aldrich show anyway?

JOEY

It probably sounds crazy but when I listen to the program I imagine what it must be like living in a single family house like he lives in with upstairs and downstairs, hot and cold water, a bathtub, your own backyard. . . Wow! You think we ' ll ever live in a place like that, Mum?

## NELLIE

You know how hard your father 's working, darling. Two jobs, the restaurant and the shipyard. He only gets about four hours' sleep. He's saving for your education and to get us a house. Who knows. . . one day you may be Henry Aldrich 's neighbor. Take your sandwich into your room and listen to your programs, and I 'm going down to see grandma before her customers start coming in. God bless her, I don ' t know where she finds the energy to do those readings every day.

> (Joey goes into the bedroom with the sandwich and sits in front of the radio. Nellie leaves the kitchen and the tenement darkens.)

# SCENE III

SETTING: Annie 's tenement lights up and reveals Annie sitting at the table with a deck of cards in her hands. She turns them over cautiously and lays them methodically in front of her.

ANNIE

(talking to herself)

Too many black cards…they're everywhere!

(She gets up and goes to the stove Where there is an old—fashioned copper coffee pot, and she starts adding some powdered coffee to it, and she's standing there when the door opens, and Nellie comes in.)

NELLIE

Hi, Mum. No one 's here yet?

ANNIE

No, sweet heart. I 'm getting ready for them. But I know I won'<sup>t</sup> t be good today. I heard that scream. Who was it this time?

NELLIE

Jimmy, Mom. Jimmy Coury.

ANNIE

Oh, my God Is it ever going to end? I 'm so worried about your brother Charlie. I thank God, every night for sending Tommy home to me. . . even the way he is. But I can 't rest until Charlie comes back

NELLIE

He'll be home soon, he said so in the letter. And I'm praying that Jimmy Coury is just missing in action and they will find him. So, don 't worry. . . By the way, where is Tommy? He can't still be sleeping.

ANNIE

Oh, yes, he came in very late last night. But at least he came home. Sometimes he 's away for two or three    days at a time.

NELLIE

Where does he go? What does he do? Is he ever going to get a job?

ANNIE

I don 't know what he does or where he goes but he acts so strange sometime. He gets so mad, he's like another person. So, I don't ask any questions. . . As far as work's concerned, he's not ready for that. It's just going to take time.

NELLIE

What about money? I know he 's hit up every friend he' ever had, and they don 't even want to see him anymore. I've given him whatever I could. He's got to be draining you. That ' s why you see that parade of people every day.

ANNIE

It 's all right, sweetheart. It's all right. There ' s
nothing I need money for. I 'm just so happy I can
do something for him. My children are my whole
life. What else do I have? I just want all of us to
be together again. You and me and Tommy and
Charlie with his new wife. Imagine! Your brother
Charlie is married, Nellie.

NELLIE

I know, Mum. Isn't it great?

ANNIE

Yes, but why did he send her home alone? Why
didn't he come with her? What's wrong with him?
I'm worried there is something she's not telling us.

NELLIE

He told you in the letter that he was all right and that
this damn war is going to be over soon. Come on. If

you read the cards, that's what you'll see, in fact, why don't you teach me how to read them? You always said it was in the blood.

You know? You never told me how you found out you could do all this stuff. . . I 'd love to know. . . Do you remember when you first found out?

ANNIE

It was a long time ago, but I do remember. I was a young girl, I was sitting with my mother on a hill on the farm we had in the old country. She pointed to the clouds that were passing by. She asked me what I could see in the different shapes they were forming in the sky. At first, I told her I could see nothing except clouds. But then she asked me to look carefully and she pointed to different areas and asked me if they looked like pictures of people or houses or animals or anything at all. After a while I began to see something that looked like a woman 's face, but the face was covered over by something. I wasn't sure if it was with long hair or what it vas, and my mother said that it was a young girl 's face that was covered over by a veil. I looked carefully at it again and said I saw what she described, and I told her, *she looks like a bride*. And my mother told me I was right that it was a bride and that bride was me. I started laughing, because I hadn't even met your father yet. But you know something, sweetheart, that same afternoon when the man who came to the farm every week from the city to see if there was anything we wanted to buy from his wagon, he had a new helper with him and that helper turned out to be your father.


NELLIE

You never told me that before, Mum. What a story!


ANNIE

Now finish your coffee and we'll turn the cups upside down for a few minutes before we read them.

(Both Nellie and Annie sip the last of the coffee and gingerly turn the demitasse cups over.)

Now while we 're waiting. Let me tell you the most important thing about fortune telling. That's watching expressions on the faces of the people you're reading for and watching any movements they make with their body or their hands while you're talking before the reading and during the reading. See how they' re dressed. If they have any jewelry on. That can tell you a lot about what they think of themselves. You'll learn that when you're doing a reading you need to do more listening than talking. In fact, my mother used to say a person tells their own fortune. . . You just underline the important parts. Remember people always want to hear the good new but, unfortunately, it's not always that way. So, you have to know how or if to tell them the bad news and how much of the bad news to tell them. You need to figure out how deep you can bring someone before you help them back up. You've always got to help them back up, sweetheart. Don 't let anyone leave a reading too depressed in fact, the reason I 'm so busy is that most people leave here happy.

Okay, turn your cup over and tell me what you see in there.

> (Nellie turns the cup and starts looking inside and after a while speaks.)
> NELLIE

I can 't make anything out of these lines, Mum.

ANNIE

Here, let me look with you. There. There see. Look
at that. Look at that shape. Like an upside-down *V*?
What does that look like to you?

NELLIE

I don't know…I can 't even guess.

ANNIE

Sure, you can. Look again. It's a rooftop. It's very
clear . That's a house, and there's shrubbery all
around. And look over there. There's another house.
And a little way down another. It's a street. Can you
see it now?

NELLIE

Now that you point it out, Mum. Yes, I can see
that. And look here. There's a drop of coffee
that's still running down the side of the cup.

ANNIE

It's a tear. But see, it's not stained too deeply. In fact,
it's almost clear. So, it's a tear of joy for your new
home, honey.

NELLIE

My new home? That's funny. That's what Joey and I were just talking about upstairs…a new home on a street with trees! I can see it now. But look, Mum, that tear is getting darker. Some of the coffee grounds are making it darker. See what I mean?

ANNIE

(She doesn't like what she sees.)

You ' re wrong We read enough in your cup. Here, look at mine and tell me what you see.

NELLIE

(looks carefully into her mother 's cup. At first you can tell from the expression on her face she's scanning and seeing nothing, but suddenly something catches her eye. She looks and then she looks at her mother and she look back in the cup.)

This is crazy. It's only because of what you told me before that I 'm seeing this. . . that must be why.

33

ANNIE

What do you mean?

NELLIE

Well, I think I see a girl "s face with what looks like it could be a veil over it. . . it really looks like that to me!

ANNIE

Let me see. . . You 're absolutely right. That ' s just what it is. It's your brother ᵗ s new wife.

(Annie becomes pensive.)

You know, her being from another country and all…it's hard for us to get used to each other. The way she dresses. Her make up. Do you think all French girls are like Simone?

NELLIE.

I don't know Mom. I know if I dressed like that, Ted would kill me. But she is really very nice, and I can tell she loves Charlie very much. I am sure she's just as confused about all of this as we are.

(Behind Annie you can see the bedroom door opening and Tommy standing there just in time to hear Annie say)

ANNIE

Nellie, sweetheart, I wish I could get Tommy to at least act civil to her. He walks out of the room whenever she comes in and he blows up at nothing!! What she must think of Tommy. He's been acting so.

TOMMY

(He quickly opens his bedroom door behind Annie)

So, what, Mum? So crazy? Is that what you were going to say? And you're worried about what that floozie Charlie married thinks of me?!!

(Nellie just stares ahead startled.)

TOMMY

Is that it, Mum?

NELLIE

(She gets from the chair and runs over to Tommy.)


No, Tommy, No! That's not what she meant at all. Was it, Mum?

ANNIE

(She gets up and tries to placate him.)
Of course not, honey. Not at all. It's just that...you know. . . the kind of hours you've been keeping and the way your temper gets the best of you sometimes, sweetheart. I'm just afraid your brother 's new wife wouldn't 't understand. That s all. I never thought for once you were crazy. It's just that you've been through so much...that's why you act a little different, sometimes...I mean anybody would.

TOMMY

How do YOU know what I've been through? Either
one of you? You don't. Nobody knows. Especially
those sons of bitches at the court martial. You know
what they tried to say I was?

ANNIE

No, no, I don't. And I don't want to know either.
Because I know it's a lie. . . whatever it is.

NELLIE

Of course, it's a lie. We know you, Tommy. There's
nothing anybody could say bad about you that we'd
believe.

TOMMY

Boy, you two are something! First, you tell me I never
talk to you about anything. And then when I'm
starting to say something, you run away from it. And
as far that piece of cheap French goods, Simone, is
concerned the less I see of her the better!!

(He turns around and starts walking into the bed— room and just before entering he turns back. . . )

Hey, Mom, after I wash up I 've got to go out. I'll need some more money, okay?

ANNIE

Sure, sure, Tommy. I don't have much now but you're welcome to it. By tonight, though, I'll have more. How about some breakfast? I'll make you something.

TOMMY

(talking from bedroom)

No, no, Mum. It's all right. I 'm not hungry.

ANNIE

You haven't been eating anything. How are you going to keep your strength up? I 'm going to fix you something.
It'll only take a minute. You can have it before you go out.

(She gets up and starts walking towards the refrigerator.)

TOMMY

(coming to doorway)

Damn it! How many times do I have to tell you, I 'm not hungry! I don't want anything to eat. Just get off my back, for Christ's sake, will you?

NELLIE

Tommy don't talk to momma like that! She's just worried about your health, that's all. What 's wrong with that?

TOMMY

You know what 's wrong with that? I'll tell you what 's wrong with that! I don't want anybody to tell me what to do! Nobody and that includes both of you, too.

(He slams the door.)

NELLIE

Why you ungrateful son of a . . .

(She's interrupted by Annie 's hand on her arm.)


ANNIE

Let him be. Nellie. He doesn't know what he' s saying. He doesn't mean any of it. Please...please, don 't get him any more nervous than he is. Come on, I'll teach you the cards like you wanted, all right? Hand them over to me.

(She takes them and pushes the deck toward Nellie.)

Cut the deck in three stacks and lay them in front of me face down. Then put your right hand over each of the stacks and make a wish. The first stack stands for your heart, the second stack stands for your home, and the third for some person that's important in your life. After you've done that, take four cards from each of the stacks and place them in front of the stack on the side that's closest to me.

(Nellie does exactly what her mother says and as she puts her hand over each stack of card and closes her eyes and makes a wish her mother watches her very intently noting that there is a subtle expression of anguish on Nellie 's face as she wishes over the third stack of cards. After the cards are placed in front of her, Annie continues)


ANNIE

I 'm going to have to go through this pretty fast because I 'm expecting some customers pretty soon. Now let's see:
the four cards for Heart. Just as I 'd expect. Here I see the eight of hearts a young person. It's got to be Joey. The king of Hearts, that's got to be Ted. The king of Diamonds and a ten of Spades. Who else could they be but your brothers. Tom is older but why is Charlie's card black? .
(She is visibly disturbed)

NELLIE

Come on, Mum. We 've got to hurry. You said you don't have much time Let's go on to the next stack.

(Reluctantly Annie puts the card down and picks up the next four. She looks at them.)

ANNIE

Here we are…old and new. The four of Hearts. The four of Diamonds. New. Young. Something new. The ten of Clubs. The jack of Spades. Older and much older. We ' re going to replace the old with the new. The old is dull, dreary, gray. But the new has lots of time to grow. Just like we saw in the coffee cup. . . Your old tenement for a new home.

NELLIE

(She murmurs half out loud)

Henry Aldrich, here we come.

ANNIE

What did you say, honey? I didn't 't hear you.

NELL.IE

Oh, nothing. Nothing. We 'd better hurry up.

> (Annie picks up the four cards
> representing the important person in
> Nellie 's life, and she looks at them,
> shoving a disapproving expression
> which she quickly eradicates from her
> face.)

ANNIE

All of these are fine, but I really haven 't got time to go over everything now. The people are coming. We'11 talk later when we have more time and I can

teach you a lot more, sweetheart

(with that Annie quickly puts the cards together and shuffles them.)

NELLIE

Are you sure everything is fine? You hardly looked at those cards.

ANNIE

Of course, I am... believe me there's nothing to worry
about. It's just that I have to start making coffee and
getting everything ready. Now, you run along. We'll
talk more about this *stuff* as you call it, later.

> (Nellie gets up and goes to the door
> looking a bit concerned. Annie gets up and
> picks up the cups and brings them over to
> the sink. When Nellie leaves, Annie turns
> from the sink and looks at the deck of cards
> and the closed door of Tommy's room and
> slowly and sadly shakes her head.)

# SCENE IV

SETTING: The stage is darkened. All you can see in the upper tenement and the area of Joey's room where there is a small green light flashing on and off.

JOEY

See, Richie. See the signal. This ring is terrific. 1 can send a code. I bet, at night, if I go to the window, you can see it from your apartment across the alley. We 've got to come up with a code. . . a secret signal.

(The lights go on and you can see the boys in the room playing with the ring.)


RICHIE

Good idea. Let 's make two long flashes and one flash mean that everything is okay.

JOEY

Okay. And three quick flashes repeated three times means I'm in danger, and you've got to come right over.

RICHIE

In danger? What kind of danger?

JOEY

How about the danger of being up here tonight with Marcia? You remember Marcia, don't you?

(He cups his hands over his chest to indicate large breasts.)

RICHIE

Oh, yeah, Marcia. I almost forgot she's coming over here tonight. You'd better flash that signal; because if you leave me out of that, you'11 be in real danger, let me tell you Joey, we've got to find some way to feel those tits and that ass. So please don 't waste too much time showing her that ring of yours. . . There's only one *secret compartment* I 'm interested in seeing.


JOEY

Nice talk. . . but you're right; it would be nice. What we 've got to do is come up with a plan that won't be too obvious. I'll think of something later. . . but right, now all I want to think about is finding the secret compartment in my ring. where do you think it is? Hou about this little lever?


RICHIE

Yeah, that must be it. just press it down.

JOEY

That's it! Did you see that small draw slide out? Look!

RICHIE

Wow! It's small alright. What can you put in there?

JOEY

A small treasure map?

RICHIE

A treasure map? Where would we ever get a treasure map?

JOEY

I was just saying that. Anything. Wait a minute. . . I know what I 'm going to put in there.

RICHIE

What? A picture from my girlie magazine so you could take it out once in a while at school or when you're by yourself, so you can get all excited?

JOEY

No, Richie. I know that 's what you 'd put in there but there's better that I want to put in there.

RICHIE

What could be better than a girl with her tits hanging out?

> (Joey starts to cough at first easily and then uncontrollably.)

RICHIE

There you go again. You haven 't been taking that medicine like your mother told you. If she hears you coughing your lungs out like that, she's going to come in here screaming at both of us.

> (Joey is still coughing uncontrollably.)

Now where is it? Where is your medicine, for Christ's sake?

(Joey points to the top of the bureau and
Richie reaches for the small bottle on
top of it, takes it, and opens it up.)
Here, take a slug of this. It always helps you. Come
on, Come on. Here

(Joey takes the bottle and tries to pour it
into the teaspoon that Richie brought with
him, but he gets frustrated with it and just
drinks from the bottle. Gradually his
coughing begins to subside, and he sits
back exhausted.)

Listen, Joey: I got it! I know what to put in that secret
compartment. The hell with the bare assed girl. Put
some of that goddamn cough medicine in there in
case you have another attack.

(Both he and Joey start to laugh.)
(Joey notices the clock and says.)


JOEY

Come on, Richie, let 's turn on the radio. It's time for
"Batman and Robin.

## SCENE V

SETTING: Ted and Nellie are in the kitchen of their tenement. The rest of the stage is dark.

TED

Now wait a minute, Nellie. You're not going to start with that voodoo witchcraft your mother does downstairs, are you? I mean I 'm kinda tired and I 'd like to get a few hours' sleep before I go to my next job. Why don't we save this for when I've got a little more time? Okay, honey?

> (We hear Joey coughing behind his closed bedroom door and Ted is about to get up and go over to Joey's room when Nellie puts her hand on his arm.)

NELLIE

Come on, Ted. This won't take long. My mom thinks I've inherited some of her gift. I just want to see if she's right. Please?

TED

(Joey's coughing subsides, and Ted turns his attention back to Nellie)

Why not? I 'm sure our future for the next ten years at least, isn't going to be much different from the last ten…I'll still be sweating my ass off behind the stove somewhere.

You know something, Nellie, I was thinking one of the craziest words in the English language is *chef* because when you hear it, it sounds like such a glamorous job…you picture a guy standing in a pure white outfit with a tall stovepipe hat adding a few spices to some fancy dish and making all kinds of money for doing it. Well, let the guy from Webster 's dictionary walk into the joint where they call me *chef.* and that bastard will change that definition fast. He'll put in it the nightmares you have about food not being delivered in time or the potato peeler not working or the refrigerator going on the blink or the short order cook or some of the other help not showing up and meanwhile the order slips keep piling up and the waitresses keep bitching about having to wait. Plus, the fact that your 've always got to be working when other people are playing. Then you've got the right definition of *chef.* There's nothing fancy about it. It's just a tired, guy, smelling of onions, coming home at the end of the week with barely enough money to keep his family going. Thank God for the shipyard job, that's all I can say.


NELLIE

Thank God is right! Not only for the extra money, but it kept you out of the service. I' m sure I would have cracked up. It was bad enough that my brothers were over there.

TED

Speaking of your brothers, Tommy was in the restaurant the other night and drinking pretty heavy. In fact, the next day the bartender told me he had started a fight. What 's with that guy, anyway? Has he ever said anything about what happened to him in army?

NELLIE

He started to when I was downstairs, but Mom stopped him.

TED

She doesn't 't really want to know, does she?


NELLIE

She keeps saying she does, but she didn't 't act it a little while ago.

(She looks up at the stove.)

Oh, the coffee 's ready.

(She fills two demitasse cups and brings them over and they start to drink.)


TED

Hey, this stuff is pretty good.

(Nellie starts smiling and they both finish their cups.)

Okay, what do I do? Turn it upside down on the saucer, right?

NELLIE

Right…and slide them over here to me.

(Nellie reaches over and takes the cup and turns it right side up and starts to peruse it.)

What a mess! This isn't going to be as easy as I thought.

TED

Why don't we stick to fortune cookies, what do you say?

NELLIE

Stop teasing. I just need a few minutes. Now, let me see. Okay, look right here. What does this look like to you?

TED

It looks like a combination shipbuilder/hash slinger who's dead tired and trying to get to bed. Pretty good, huh?

NELLIE

Oh, come on. Be serious? It doesn't look like that at all.

TED

No? Well, then what does it look like, oh, seer of all things?

NELLIE

(She laughs lightly.)
I see two figures here.

TED

Maybe the guy isn't as tired as I thought, and he's trying to get his wife in the bedroom with him.
(He looks at her slyly.)

NELLIE

If that's really what you see in there, then I should have started this earlier.

TED

Very funny. Very funny. I think the caffeine is getting to you.

(He's interrupted by the coughing coming from Joey's room and they both look at each other but Nellie quickly diverts her attention to the inside of the coffee cup.)

NELLIE

Hold on. Look over here. See these two lines?

They rejoin up here. I should have recognized it. It's a house, but it 's shaped differently. It's much larger than the ones I saw downstairs. . . That's why I didn't 't recognize it right away. It's the only one in sight. There are a lot of things around it. It could be trees. Yeah, it could be a house in the country. And there are two objects in front of the building. They look like people. One is tall, and one is small. It could be a man and his wife or maybe a parent and a child. Maybe it's you and Joey. But what 's the building? It's not a school. There are no other buildings around it. Oh, my God! Ted, it's a sanitorium. Ted, you 're taking Joey to a sanitorium! That's what you've always said you were going to do and there it is. You 're planning on doing it. You're planning on taking him away.

> (Nellie breaks down and Ted comes around to her side of the table and puts his hands on her shoulders trying to cornfort her.)

TED

Nellie, I don 't know how come you decided to do this now. You've always known that Joey was going to have to end up in a sanitorium sooner or later. All that business about his just having a weakness is just a lot of wishful thinking What you did just now is read your own mind. You said what you saw in the cup was a parent and a child.

That's really you holding Joey's hand. Because deep down you know that's the best thing for him. But if you want me to play the heavy, I will. Yes, it's me in there taking Joey to the sanitarium. And the way he been sounding lately, we can't wait much longer. We've got to do something soon.

(She lifts her head from the table and
wipes the tears with her hands and
becomes almost indignant.)


NELLIE

You 're talking nonsense again! Do you think
there's any way in the world I would let you or
anybody take Joey away from me?

TED

Nellie, I don't want to take him away from you.
Remember he's my son, too. I just want what 's best
for him.  Look more carefully into that cup of
yours, and you Il see that sanitarium also has an exit
door. You'll see two figures walking out, but this
time the small one isn't so small anymore and he's
not as frail. He's taller and stronger. If you'll look
again, Nellie, that [1]s what you'll see.

(He takes the cup and puts it in
front of Nellie 's face and Nellie swings
her hand to push the cup away and it
falls to the floor and breaks.)

NELLIE

Oh, my God! That beautiful cup my mother gave to us.

(She goes to the floor and tries to pick up the pieces.)


TED

That's right, Nellie. Let's concentrate on the broken cup. Let's push everything else out of our minds for a little while longer.

(He looks down at the table.)

Hey, Nellie, you haven't read your cup yet. Here, let me do it for you. You know what I see in here. I see a work horse. No, on second thought, it looks more like a jackass who's trying to kick his way out of the tenement house but all he does is land in the tenement below him. And on his back, he's got this beautiful girl and a beautiful little boy and he's trying to carry them to some nice place far away but he keeps ending up in a place just like he left except each time he's just a little more cut up and a little more dirty but he's also a little more determined to carry the people he loves away from all this shit. . . but only after he rests for a while. Come on. . . we'll pick up the pieces later.

(He reaches down and takes her hand and leads her towards the bedroom as she 's wiping her eyes.)

# SCENE VI

SETTING: Joey's room at about 7:00 p. m. Joey is sitting in front of the radio. In the background, you can hear the theme for *The Lone Ranger*. Richie is lying on the bed thumbing through his magazine, paying no attention at all to the radio program. We hear the announcer say:

*AS YOU WILL REMEMBER, BOYS AND GIRLS, AT THE END OF LAST WEEK'S EPISODE, WE LEFT TONTO TIED AND GAGGED AT THE HIDEAWAY OF THE RUTHLESS OUTLAW SCARFACE WILLIE. . . SCAR-FACE WAS HEATING AN IRON POKER IN HIS COAL BURNING STOVE AND THREATENING TONTO. . . IF HE DIDN'T REVEAL THE WHEREABOUTS OF THE LONE RANGER'S SECRET CAVE, HE WAS GOING TO STICK THE RED-HOT POKER INTO TONTO UNTIL HE GAVE SCARFACE THE LOCATION.*

### RICHIE

I wonder what it feels like?

JOEY

Are you kidding? It's gonna hurt. ...it's so hot.

RICHIE

Yeah, it's hot all right. But do you think it's gonna hurt for long?


JOEY

Well, I suppose it depends on where you stick it.

RICHIE

Oh, wow! I just got a wild thought!


JOEY

I remember reading about a girl who fainted when she saw some guy coming at her with a long, hot iron rod.

RICHIE

Yeah? That must have been some crazy guy!

JOEY

Oh, he was. in fact, that guy not only had the one he
heated up in the fireplace…he was hold his own rod
in his hand.

RICHIE

You are a sex maniac.

(He is interrupted by Nellie opening the
door to bring Marcia in.)

NELLIE

Here 's a lovely young lady to see you. boys.

(The boys are obviously excited to see her.)

JOEY

Hi, Marcia. Come sit down with us. We're listening
to *The Lone Ranger*.

RICHIE

Yeah, come sit here between us, Marcia.

(He makes room but not too much room. Marcia seductively squirms down between them. )


NELLIE

(leaving)
Have fun.

(We now can hear the radio announcer)

*WE WILL RETURN TO THE
ADVENTURES OF THE LONE
RANGER AND TONTO RIGHT AFTER
THIS MESSAGE FROM CHEERIOS.
REMEMBER, BOYS AND GIRLS, YOU
ONLY GOT TWO WEEKS LEFT TO
SEND AWAY FOR YOUR SIGNAL
DECODER RING WITH THE SECRET
COMPARTPENT.*


MARCIA

(She's a seductive, well-endowed
adolescent girl who 's poured herself into
a sweater. She's also wearing a skirt,

white and brown saddle shoes and bobby socks.)

Isn't that the ring you told me you had, Joey?

(While she's talking both the boys are sitting on the floor either side of her having a difficult time taking their eyes off her chest.)

JOEY

It sure is. Want to see I've got it right here in my pocket.

MARCIA

Oh, I 'd love to. Wouldn't 't you, Richie?

RICHIE

Oh, yes, I'd love to see them. . . I mean it.

MARCIA

(catches Richie 's slip and smiles coyly while she takes a deep breath to stretch her sweater almost to the breaking point and Richie sort of turns to the audience with an *Oh, my God!* look.)


JOEY .

Here it is. Here's the ring. Isn't it a beauty? Look here 's the secret compartment. Just press this little lever and the draw comes out.


MARCIA

Oh, isn't that adorable! It's the cutest little box I 've ever seen.

RICHIE

Oh, I bet it. is.


JOEY

That's not all. It actually glows in the dark.

MARCIA

Oh, you've got to show me, Joey. Please show me.

JOEY

I 'd love to, but Richie 's so afraid of the dark that sometimes he faints.

RICHIE

What the hell are you talking about?

> (Marcia turns toward him and doesn't see Joey give Richie the high sign that if he faints, he'll *faint* on top of Marcia. Richie catches on quickly and continues.)

Oh, that's right, Marcia. I never know what I 'm going to do when I 'm in the dark. It 's almost like something over takes me.

MARCIA

Oh, Richie. Don't be afraid. I'll be here to protect you, but I really do want to see the ring shine in the dark. Please? What do you say, Richie? Please.

RICHIE

Okay, but I 'm warning you I'm not responsible for what happens. My mother said it's a phobia.

MARCIA

Phobia? What's a phobia, Richie?

RICHIE

I don't really know exactly, but it's when you're so afraid of something that if you go near it, strange things can happen. . . I think my cousin Shirley is a phobia.

MARCIA

What do you mean?

RICHIE

Well, the other morning I heard the iceman talking to someone, and he told them that he would never go out with my cousin Shirley again because he was afraid of her. From the way he was talking it sounded like he went out with her, and something very strange happened to the plumbing in his house.

JOEY

The plumbing in his house? What do you mean?

RICHIE

Well, he said ever since his date with Shirley, he's
had some kind of drip.

JOEY

Forget about your cousin Shirley. Come on, let 's
turn the light out and look at the ring. Marcia, get
close to Richie. Okay?

MARCIA

Okay.

JOEY

(pulls the light switch and the room
darkens)

Now look carefully, you two. Here, I 've got the ring
in my hand. See how it glows?

MARCIA

Oh, yes! I do see it. How beautiful! Isn't it beautiful, Richie?

RICHIE

Oh, yes. Oh, wait. Oh, my God! Marcia, I'm going to faint. I 'm going to faint!

MARCIA

Joey, help me. He's landed right on top of me.

JOEY

Don 't worry about a thing. I '11 be right there to help you.

MARCIA

What shall I do?

JOEY

Mouth to mouth resuscitation. That's what you 've got to do. You've got to put your mouth on his mouth and start breathing for him. He's unconscious.

RICHIE

Yeah, yeah. That's the only thing that helps me, Marcia. Open your mouth and put it on mine.

MARCIA

How the hell can he be unconscious if he's talking to me?

JOEY

Oh, he's delirious. Yeah, that's it! He's delirious.

MARCIA

Oh, yeah. Well, I 'm not delirious. He's getting no mouth to mouth from me. What's he doing with his hands?

JOEY

He must be having a seizure. He shakes all over when he's having a seizure.


MARCIA

I don 't know what it is, but he better stops.

JOEY

Here, let me help you.


MARCIA

That's some help, Joey. You must be having a seizure, too, huh? All right, you two, that's enough. Get the lights on. I 've had enough of things that glow and things that grope and there are even some things that are beginning to grow in the dark. . . I gotta tell you if it can cause all that. . . that's some ring you've got there.

JOEY

You don' t understand, Marcia. It's just that Richie 's scared stiff.

MARCIA

He's stiff all right. And if you don't turn the light
on, he's going to have a hell of a lot more than the
dark to be scared of. I didn't tell you that my brother
Gino is home from the Marines.

JOEY

Oh, oh. All right. Don't worry about a thing. As
soon as I can squeeze myself out of here, I'll turn
the light on.

MARCIA

Never mind, I'll do it myself.

(Marcia gets up, turns the light on, and is standing
holding the string and you can see Richie on top of
Joey and Richie is moaning with his eyes closed)

RICHIE

Marcia, Marcia, I love you! You're so beautiful!

JOEY

(yelling)

Will you get the hell off me, Richie?

RICHIE

Oh, my God! How did you get here?

(Richie falls back and sits propped against the wall and sees Marcia.)

RICHIE

See, I told you crazy. things happen to me in the dark.

MARCIA

Crazy things were happening to me in the dark, too. Boy, you two guys are a pair of losers. How long did it take you to think up that stupid scheme?

JOEY

Come on, Marcia. You ain't no saint. So, get off your high horse. Don 't tell us that you didn't 't feel anything, even a little something.

MARCIA

Oh, yeah, I felt a couple of little somethings and I 'm not saying that I didn't 't enjoy it. But that's not the way that it's done.


RICHIE

No, Marcia? How about showing us the way it's done. . . what do you say?

MARCIA

(after some deliberation)

All right, I'll show you, and I do want the lights out. But I don 't want to hear any more baloney about your
phobias or seizures or the rest of that crap.


RICHIE

No, no, I promise. Just show us what to do. Joey and I are all   yours.

MARCIA

Okay. You lie down in front of me here. And, Joey, after you put the light out, you come lie down next to him.

RICHIE

(does what Marcia says)

Like this, Marcia? Is this okay?

. MARCIA

Yeah, fine…fine.

RICHIE

Hurry up, Joey. Hurry up. Turn off the goddamn light.
JOEY

Okay, hold your horses. I 'm hurrying.

(puts the light out and the stage is in darkness)

RICHIE

(after while)

Oh, Marcia! Marcia! I don't know what your 're doing.

MARCIA

Shut up!

RICHIE

But it feels terrific.


JOEY

Yeah, yeah. Me, too. Wow! That's nice, Marcia. That's nice.

RICHIE

Marcia, you re kinda heavy. Could you just....Marcia, I 'm having a hard time breathing. Marcia, move off just a little bit.

JOEY

Oh, she just rolled over on me, Oh, it feels good Marcia, but could you move your elbow?

## RICHIE

Yeah, and your foot! Your foot. It's in my mouth! Stop kicking, Marcia.

## JOEY

Jesus, Richie. I think this time she's having a seizure!

## RICHIE

Marcia, you better slow down a little. It's beginning to hurt. It's beginning to hurt a lot. Marcia, can you slow down, please? Oh, wait. Take it easy, Marcia. Your teeth, Marcia, your teeth! Have you still got braces on? Oh, my God! Joey, you've got to get her off me.

## JOEY

I can't do much. She's got one knee in my rib cage and the other one…you know where!

RICHIE

Joey, please put the light on. Please! I can 't take any
more of this. She's going crazy.

(Just then you can hear the sirens outside)

JOEY

I can 't, Richie. I can 't.

RICHIE

What do you mean you can ' t?

JOEY

That    was the signal for the blackout. I can't turn
the light on.

RICHIE

Oh, shit. Please, Joey, please! Turn them on. I'd
rather take my chances with the goddamn krauts
than this piranha.

JOEY

I can't, Richie, and besides her mother is the air raid
warden.

Can you imagine if she ever came up and saw this. .
. that's enough, Marcia. For Christ's sake, stop it,
will you?

> (He begins to cough, first slowly, then
> violently.)


RICHIE

Oh, God! Joey, you've got to get your medicine.
Marcia, stop it! Can't you hear Joey?

MARCIA

What 's wrong? God, he sounds like he's going to die.

RICHIE

It's that weakness of his. It's getting worse. Damn
it, I 've got to find that medicine.

MARCIA

Well, where is it?

RICHIE

On top of the bureau, and we can't put the light on, so we '11 have to do it by feel. You're an expert at that, Marcia. Why don't you give me a hand?

MARCIA

This is no time for wisecracks. I don't like the way Joey sounds.

RICHIE

It's the worst I've ever heard him. I know this room by heart. It should just be over here. Good, I've got it. Joey, I've got the medicine. Just hold on a minute. Here it is.

(After a few minutes you can hear Joey's cough subsiding. The lights go on.)

RICHIE

That was the worst...pal, wasn't it?

JOEY

(exhausted)

Yeah, it was the worst. It was the first time I thought it would never stop. Thank God the blackout ended. I've never been afraid of the dark before, but I was this time.

# ACT 11

## SCENE 1

SETTING: The stage is dark except for Annie ' s apartment, and she's sitting at the table in front of two elderly sisters. The oldest very masculine and the younger is very feminine and trying every way to look even younger. Only the younger one is having her fortune told as the older sister sits protectively and expressing discouragement and a disbelief of any comments in the reading that even hint of something or someone that may take the younger sister away from her.

### ANNIE

(looking into the cup of the younger sister)

I see you standing in a field with lots of flowers and the sun is shining on your pretty clothes. Right behind you is a large boulder. It's got a funny shape. . . it's got a big chip on it. It almost looks like someone I 've seen before

(glances up at Bella)

wait a minute. . . I see something . . . .like someone 's head peeking around that rock...
Yes, that's what it is. It's somebody that's admiring you.

DELIA

Oh let me see! What does he look like? Is he handsome?

ANNIE

Here, look here. See, this is you. And the field. And there's that funny shaped boulder behind you.

> (With each reference to this rock or boulder, Annie glances towards Bella, and the older sister shifts uncomfortably in her chair.)

DELIA

Yes, I see that. But where's the man? That handsome man who wants me?

ANNIE

Wait a minute now. I didn't say anything about what he wants or what he looks like. But look right there...see
that's somebody's head looking at you.

DELIA

(straining, looking)
Yes, I do see him, and he is very handsome.


BELLA

(quickly grabs the cup from her sister's hands)
Let me see. There's nothing in there. Just a bunch of coffee grounds. You're both crazy.

DELIA

Oh, you moved the cup too quickly. You must have ruined it. Let me see. Oh, you did! She did! Look.

ANNIE

Yes, everything looks different in here now. I'm afraid I can't tell YOU anything more.

DELIA

Oh, but you've got to. You've got to tell me more!

Doesn't she, Bella? Doesn't she?

BELLA

She's filled your head with enough nonsense.

(Reaching into her jacket, she pulls out two quarters.)

Here's your fifty cents, Annie. Delia and I are going to get out of here.

DELIA

Isn't there any way you could tell me more about that man, Annie? Please! I know you're right about someone admiring me. I can feel it. I can feel it.

BELLA

What do you feel? Where do you feel it?

DELIA

Deep inside me.

BELLA

(standing up)

That's it! That's enough. Let 's get out of here.

DELIA

No! No! I must know more. Please, Annie, please! I'll pay you anything you want. Just tell me, tell me more.

ANNIE

That means we'll have to read the cards.

BELLA

How much will that cost?

ANNIE

A dollar. It takes a lot of energy, you understand.

BELLA

That's not all it takes a lot of.


DELIA

Be quiet, Bella. Annie, can't you find something to keep her busy?

ANNIE .

Come to think of it, Bella, you could do me a favor. Just wait a minute.

> (Annie goes to the refrigerator and comes back with two plastic bags filled with a white Crisco-like material.)

Here, Bella. You could squeeze the color into these margarine bags for me. That'll save me a little time before tonight's dinner. You don't mind, do you?

DELIA

Mind? Massaging those things is right up her alley.

BELLA

Very funny. Just put them down, Annie, and if I feel up to it. . . I 'll do it.

DELIA

Annie, please go ahead. . . I can't wait any longer. Please. . .

> (Annie starts laying down the cards in front of her. Five down. Eight across. The younger sister can't control her excitement while Bella obviously exhibits her skepticism.)

ANNIE

There now. That's forty cards. That leaves us with twelve. I want you to take four cards from the twelve, Delia, and place them face down in front of me.

DELIA

Of course, anything. . . I'll do anything you say.

(Delia anxiously picks four cards out, places them in front of Annie.)

There! Now tell me about that tall, dark, handsome man standing behind the boulder with the crack in it?

BELLA
(indignantly)

She said the boulder had a chip on it. She didn't
't say anything about a crack

(She picks up one of the Oleomargarine bags.)

DELIA

Go on Annie, please.

ANNIE

I usually get paid before I go any further, you understand.

BELLA

No, I don 't understand. I don't understand any of this.

DELIA

Pay her. Pay her, Bella. I don't understand you today. I 'm going to be very angry with you. And you know how mean I can get when I get angry?

BELLA

All right, Deedee. Don't get mad. Please, don 't get mad. Here 's your dollar, Annie. And remember all she wants to hear about is that creep! And no more cracks, I mean remarks, about that boulder. All right?

(She starts squeezing the bag vigorously.)


ANNIE

(taking the dollar)

Bella, all I do is read the cards. I have no control over the powers that are directing your sister 's future love life.

DELIA

Did you hear that, Bella? *My love life*! I knew when I saw that man 's face that he would be insatiable. But I 'll try my best to satisfy him.

BELLA

Would you believe it? She's turning a coffee grind into Rudolph Valentino!!

DELIA

Bella, remember what I told you! Go on, Annie, tell me about my lover, and how much he's longing for me.

ANNIE

(looking over the field of cards in front of her)

Now let 's gee. Ah, here you are? Right in the middle of all these hearts and diamonds.

DELIA

Hearts and diamonds! You hear that, Bella? Hearts and diamonds!

BELLA

Yeah, I heard already. I heard!

DELIA

Which one am I, Annie? Which one?

ANNIE

Here, the ten of hearts.

DELIA

Oh, the ten. I thought I 'd be the queen.

ANNIE

Oh, no, my dear. That 's much too old for you.

DELIA

Of course, Annie. You 're absolutely right. I wasn't thinking. What about the eight of hearts, Annie? Isn't that even closer to my age?

BELLA

How about the joker?

DELIA

Bella, you 'd better take a good look at these cards. Because when you get home, you're going to be playing a lot of solitaire! Don't pay any attention to her, Annie. Please go on. . . And I think you're perfectly right about the ten of hearts because I know my future husband wants not only a passionate but a mature woman.

ANNIE

Now let 's see what else the cards tell us. If you look at the field of cards, there are two picture cards of your suit, the jack and the king, that have still not been turned over. And you may have handed one or both of them to me in these four cards. I hope you only handed me the king.

DELIA

Why? What happens if I 've given you both?

ANNIE

Well, I have to put any picture card of your suit right on your card. The king of hearts, of course, represents the man who is in love with you.

DELIA

And that means if you turn his card over, you're going to lay him on top of me?

ANNIE

Well, I suppose you could put it that way.

DELIA

Ok, but if he's there, Annie, lay him on me gently please, firmly but gently.

BELLA

(starts singing looking down at the Oleo bag as she works it)

And you'll spread your wings and you'll take to the sky.

(The younger sister turns and glares at Bella.)

I was just singing to the music on the radio.

DELIA

Well, spare us, huh? Ella Fitzgerald, you ' re not. A hoarse Caruso, maybe.

> (An unequivocal sneer passes from Bella to Delia.)

DELIA

Now, let 's see. Where were we? I think you were just putting my king of hearts gently in me. I mean on me. Isn't that right?

ANNIE

Not exactly, Delia. I was just about to turn the cards and see what we had. We'll have to hurry. I have other people coming this afternoon.

> (Annie turns the first card over.)

Nine of hearts.

DELIA

What does that mean, Annie? The nine of hearts?

ANNIE

(barely looking up)

Competition.

DELIA

Younger competition

(with emphasis on younger).

ANNIE

(turns over the next card)

The eight of clubs.

BELLA

I bet that means a young black horny girl.

(She picks up the second bag and squeezes one in each hand.)

DELIA

Bella, this is my fortune, not yours.

ANNIE

The eight of clubs just means that things aren't perfectly smooth in the relationship.

DELIA

Oh, maybe, just a lover's quarrel. You know how temperamental those Latin men are.

BELLA

Or maybe it just means he has a small case of gonorrhea or syphilis.

DELIA

Bella, will you shut up and squeeze your bags!!

ANNIE

Ladies! Ladies! We must go on. You're not my only clients this afternoon.

(Annie turns the next card.)

The jack of hearts. There's somebody other than the king after you.

DELIA

Not to worry. There's enough to go around! Mother always said God-give gifts are to be shared. Didn't she, Bella?

BELLA

No comment

(playing the bags)

ANNIE

(turning the last card)

Well, look here. The king of hearts. But it's too late.

DELIA

What do you mean, *too late*, Annie?

ANNIE

There's already somebody covering you. The king of hearts goes right on top. But there's somebody between you two. . . the jack.

DELIA

(She stands up abruptly and angrily.)

It's not a jack that's between us.

(She glares at Bella and starts to cry. Bella squeezes one bag so hard she bursts it. Just then there's a knock at the kitchen door. ⟩

ANNIE

I'm sorry, but that's my next customer. Why don't you two leave by the back door?

(She hands Bella a towel to wipe herself on the way out. After they leave, Annie quickly puts the cards back into a deck, shouting)
One minute, please.

(Annie opens the door and gees Father Elixir. )

ANNIE

Father! What a surprise! I haven't seen you for a long time!

FATHER ELIXIR

That's one of the reasons I 've come to see you,
Annie.

ANNIE

Oh, Father, you know I 've meant to get to church,
but I've got this arthritis. I never know when it's
going to kick up. Come in and have a cup of coffee.

FATHER ELIXIR

Thank you, Annie. I really do have something I
want to talk to you about.

ANNIE

It's not bad news…is it, Father? You haven't heard
anything about my boy, have you?

FATHER ELIXIR

Oh, no, no! Nothing like that. No, it's not that kind
of bad news.

ANNIE

What kind is it, Father? Tell me I'm not worried. I'm a good woman. Maybe not a second Mother Cabrini, but I 'd be able to convince St. Peter to let me squeeze through those gates.

(Annie goes to the stove, pours the coffee, serves it, and sits down opposite Father Elixir.)

FATHER ELIXIR

Annie, I 've heard from a number of the parishioners that you 're telling fortunes. Now you know as well as I do that telling fortunes, even playing cards for any money, is frowned upon by the church. Is it true? If it is, what have to say for yourself?

ANNIE

*What have I got to say for myself, Father*? I'll tell you what I 've got to say for myself. You know the expression: *God will provide*? Well, God has provided me with a gift to support myself. And I'd be acting against God 's will if I ignored that. I don't read the cards or the coffee grinds, Father, I read the people. And depending on what I see in them, I give the best advice I can. Come on, let me show you, Father.

FATHER ELIXIR

What do you mean? You 're going to tell my fortune?

ANNIE

No, let say I 'm going to confession to you, *my way*. I 'm going to show you what I do, and you determine if it's a sin or not and what my penance will be. What do you say? You can 't deny me the sacrament.

FATHER ELIXIR .

(looks around to assure himself they're alone)

If you put it that way, Annie, I haven't got much choice. .

ANNIE

Here, take the cards... do you even know how to shuffle them?

(Father takes the cards and first intentionally shuffles them awkwardly and slowly but then shuffles them very expertly. In fact, too expertly for a man who just said card playing was a sin. Annie smiles.)

Father, before we start let me make another cup of coffee. Or better still, how about a little sherry? You sound a little congested to me.

FATHER ELIXIR

(looking at his watch)

Well, it is a little early but (coughing slightly and sniffing), I think I am coming down with something.

ANNIE

Then the sherry will help you...please cut the deck into three piles while I get the drinks.

> (While she goes to the kitchen cabinet and gets a bottle and a couple of glasses, Father continues some quick, fancy shuffling and ends up with three separate piles of cards on the table all face down. Annie is behind him holding the glasses and bottle. After watching these cardshark-like maneuvers, Annie smiles and silently claps her hands together as if to say: *THIS IS GOING TO BE FUN.* She comes around and sets her glass by her side and one by the priest's side.)

Sorry, Father. I can't find the sherry. But here's a bottle of brandy that one of

my grateful clients gave me. I've been waiting for a special occasion to open it, and I can't

think of a better time. Would you do the
honors, please?


FATHER ELIXIR

Of course. Allow me. H-m-m, seventeen-
year old, 100 proof...

> (He picks up the bottle and peruses the
> label with interest and delight, then
> opens the bottle and pours Annie a
> drink and himself an equal measure.
> Then he looks up and thinking that
> Annie is paying no attention to him, he
> pours himself an extra inch   or so.
> Annie again nods knowing she now
> has enough ammunition to make this
> an interesting reading.)

ANNIE

(picks up her glass to toast with

the priest) Bless me, Father, for I'm

about to sin.

> (They both start to laugh, and she
> sips her drink while the priest downs
> half of his.)

ANNIE

This is going to be a little unusual because
one of the piles is usually dedicated to
affairs of the heart. But that's not
appropriate in your case, is it, Father? The
second to home, and the Church is your home,
but the third is dedicated to someone that's
very important in your life. Let's
concentrate on that one. So now you have a
choice. You pick one of the piles and put it
in front of me.

(He hesitates over one of the piles and then
moves

to another and pushes it in front of
Annie.)

Fine, fine. Now while I'm arranging these
cards, please help yourself to some more
brandy. You obviously shortchanged
yourself. And I really don't like the way
you sound. I don't care how old you are.
There are times when you need someone to
take care of you and tell you what to do.

(The priest gently taps his throat and
coughs a

bit and refills his glass--this
time to the brim.)

Sip a bit of that, Father. Before it spills.
It's too good to waste.

(The priest obliges willingly.)

Let's see. We're going to take every third card from this pile and place it face up to get some idea of this important person in your life.

> (When she starts to do this, she picks up her glass and sips and nods toward the priest to join her. When she finishes, she sips again. This time the priest nearly finishes his glass.)

Interesting. Very interesting. Most of these cards are kings and jacks.

FATHER ELEXIR

What does that mean?

ANNIE

They're all men. It a man that very important to you.

FATHER ELIXIR

It's God. It's Christ. It's my late father. You don't have to be a mind reader to come to that conclusion.

ANNIE

No, these are all hearts and diamonds. That represents someone that's living. Someone that' here. And because they're mostly hearts, you're very close to this person emotionally.

FATHER ELIXIR

What are you trying to say?

ANNIE

This man doesn't have to be another person. He could be another aspect of yourself. Another dimension of your personality or some talent maybe that you've never been willing to talk about or expose publicly.

(The priest takes the bottle of brandy and pours himself another drink and lights a cigarette (optional and starts puffing nervously).

The only queen here is the queen of clubs which means that there was a woman that was important to you but she's dead. She knew about this talent you had, and she wanted you to develop it, but she died. Maybe while you were still young.

(The priest starts to loosen his Roman collar and begins to nod his head slowly, sadly, and the effect of the brandy is becoming obvious in his actions and in his speech.)

FATHER ELIXIR

    (as he fills his glass)

My mother. You're talking about my mother.
She knew all about it and how good I was.
How good I still am. But my father, that son
of a bitch! *No! No!* The theater was just full
of whores and bums, not a place for his son.

But I knew he was spending his whole life
whoring and drinking. The only reason he
didn't want me in the theater, he thought I'd
catch him there with some floozie. I've never
forgiven him.


ANNIE

    (not wanting him to get any more
    emotional)

Tell me about this talent of yours.
Singing? Acting? What?


FATHER ELIXIR

Dancing, Annie, dancing!

ANNIE

Dancing! Well, well, isn't that wonderful? Oh, I bet you were a good dancer. What about your mother? Was she a good dancer, too?

FATHER ELIXIR

Oh, she was a wonderful dancer. When I was a little boy, I remember hearing the Glenn Miller and Artie Shaw bands playing on the radio after my mother thought I had fallen asleep. She always played the radio when she was alone which means she played the radio very often. I would sneak out of bed and walk quietly over to the bedroom door which was closed but never locked; and I'd push it open very slightly--just enough for me to be able to see into the kitchen and there I'd see my mother dancing in the arms of her make-believe partner--twirling, dipping, gliding across the linoleum so gracefully that her plain cotton housedress became transformed before my very eyes into one of the lovely flowing chiffon dresses Ginger Rogers would always wear in the movies my mother used to take me to each week. Oh, she loved those musicals!! And I did, too; because every time I looked at my mother's face during the movie, she was smiling, and she was happy. I never saw my mother look like that at home except, of course, at night when she was dancing. I'd watch her until the radio show was over. Then the chiffon turned back to cotton, and I went reluctantly back to bed. My mother would sit quietly somewhere waiting for my father, and, perhaps wondering, if he would come home at all that night.

ANNIE

Well, how did you learn to dance?

FATHER ELIXIR

My mother taught me. One night while she was dancing in the kitchen, I tried to imitate some of the steps I had seen in the movies. But it was dark in the bedroom, and one of my Fred Astaire leaps landed me against the night table, and the lamp came crashing down. My mother rushed into the bedroom; and when I explained what had happened, we both started laughing. She said that since I was up anyway, it was silly for her to be dancing all by herself and that I would make a perfectly wonderful dancing partner. So, she taught me.

ANNIE

You both must have had a
          wonderful time.
FATHER ELIXIR

Annie, you have no idea. Nothing was more important to me than that hour each night except, of course, for going to the movie each week to learn some new routine. We got so that we could do every dance. And then, after a while, we began to choreograph our own. It was wonderful.

(He points to the bottle.)

Just a drop more? Do you mind?

ANNIE

Not at all. Did anyone ever see you two dance together?


FATHER ELIXIR

Oh, yes. The first time was the church variety show at Christmas time. We were such a hit that it became an annual event. The really big break came one summer when we heard they were having casting tryouts in Boston for a new musical. Mom managed to get the train fare together from the little allowance my father would give her whenever he showed up, and we headed into town. What a day, Annie! I'll never forget it. I had on a new suit I had bought for the previous Easter, and Mom bought a pattern and made herself the prettiest dress I have ever seen... the skirt went way out whenever she turned. What a team we were!

ANNIE

Oh, I bet you both were so excited. Come on, tell me what happened?

FATHER ELIXIR

Well, it's a good thing we got the early train because it was a long walk to the theater, and we couldn't afford a cab. When we finally got there, the auditions had already started so we sat in the back of the theater, and we watched. Goodness, there were some excellent dancers; but the more I watched them the less nervous I became, because I knew we were better. And by the time they called us up to the stage, we both were ready. I can hear the music now, *"Dancing in the Dark."* We had done that number a hundred times before, and we flowed so smoothly and easily across that stage that when it was over, we heard some applause from the few people that were sitting in the theater.

ANNIE

So, you two got the part? How wonderful!


FATHER ELIXIR

Well, we both didn't get the part. The director said he needed me but that my mother was a little too old for the role he had in mind. Well, I told him right then and there we were a team. He either took both of us or the deal was off. Imagine! Saying that my mother was too old! She wasn't old at all, Annie. You should have seen that face! The way her body moved to the music and responded so easily into any step I would lead her.

## ANNIE

That director must have been crazy. He didn't know what he was talking about! How did your mother react?

## FATHER ELIXIR

Well, she surprised me, Annie. She told me right in front of the director that what he said was right. That she only came down so that my talent could be showcased, and she never wanted to appear on the stage. And besides, she said that during the routine we had just performed, she somehow had sprained her left ankle, and she knew it would take a long time before she'd be able to dance again. She insisted that I take the part and wouldn't leave until I agreed. It was strange, Annie. All during the routine and afterwards when we walked off the stage and down into the audience to meet the director, I never noticed anything wrong with

my mother's leg. But right after I
accepted the part and we started to
leave the theater for the train station,
she began to walk with a limp, and
the limp never went away. Never. She
was never able to dance with me
again. She said it was arthritis. You
know, Annie, that's a terrible
disease. It can come on so quickly
like that.


ANNIE

Oh, you're right. You're absolutely
right. I'm full of arthritis. So, I can
understand how much hurt she felt. It
must have been hard on both of
you. But now I want to hear about
the Boston musical. I bet you were
terrific.

# FATHER ELIXIR

Oh, it was a lot of hard work, Annie. The choreographer was tough. But she liked my work, and, in fact, she made me an understudy for one of the bigger parts promising that if anything went wrong, she'd move me out of the chorus. But it wasn't only tough physically. It was becoming nearly impossible financially. The few dollars they were paying me just took care of my transportation. Some days if I'd forgotten to bring a lunch I just went Without eating. I never told Mum that, of course. I told

her that everything was just fine. But when enough mornings went by when she couldn't get up early enough to make a sandwich or there really wasn't much to make it with, hunger made me desperate.

ANNIE

So, what did you do? Get a job?

FATHER ELIXIR

No, I didn't have time. But there was a lot
of time during rehearsals and the stage
manager and some of the guys started playing
poker. Well, as you know, there's a lot of
card playing around this neighborhood. And
besides, the ones thing my father ever taught
me was how to play poker. I used to go to
the coffee houses and watch him "*take the
suckers*" as he used to say. Those card
games kept him away from the house so
much that I swore I'd never play card. But
when it became my only opportunity to
make a few dollars, I put my second talent to
use. And then I started "*taking the suckers*"

but only for as much as I needed to get by
until opening night.

ANNIE

Opening night! That had to be exciting!
Your mother must have enjoyed it so much.


FATHER ELIXIR

She never got there.

ANNIE

Her arthritis was so bad, huh? I know it can get

pretty uncomfortable.

FATHER ELIXIR

No, it wasn't her arthritis. The night before
when I came home from dress rehearsal she
was in bed, and she looked terrible. Her face

was swollen on one side, and she was covered with black and blue welts, and there was still some crusted blood in one nostril. I asked her what happened, and she told me she had fallen. I didn't believe her. I asked her if my father had come home. She told me he hadn't; but when I looked in the closet, I saw the one

suitcase we owned was missing and some of his things were gone from the closet. She was so weak even the next day she had trouble swallowing. I told her I wasn't going to go to opening night, but she insisted. She insisted that I go. I'll never forget that train ride into Boston that afternoon. I was so angry and so worried. I thought I'd never be able to perform on stage. But I did. The critics loved the show, but I didn't even stay for the opening night party. I got on the milk train from Boston; and when I got home, the neighbors and the doctor were there. And the priest had gotten there in time to give her the Last Rites. But I was too late, Annie. She was already dead when I got to her side. I wasn't with my mother when she died, Annie; I was up there on the stage dancing. I've never been able to forgive myself or my father. It's ironic, isn't it? I entered the priesthood to be able to administer the sacraments, but I haven't been able to even consider granting my father absolution or accepting it for myself. There's something really wrong about that, isn't there, Annie?

ANNIE

As I see it, Father, you've committed no sin that you have to be absolved from. And as far as your father goes, he probably has already dealt with his part in all of this, his own way. And you want to know what else I think of all this? I don't think you were separated from your mother one minute that opening night. She was sitting front row center proudly applauding and having the best time.

FATHER ELIXIR

Do you think so, Annie? Do you really think
so? Oh, I'd give anything to believe that.


ANNIE

Well, she was. She was because you were so
good. Oh, I would have done anything to see
you up there on that stage. Too bad you can't
dance anymore.


FATHER ELIXIR

Who said I can't dance anymore, Annie? I told
you I can still out dance Fred Astaire and
Gene Kelly. Here let's turn on the radio, and
I'll show you.


(He stands up, takes off his jacket,
exposing his pot belly. His Roman

collar is half on. He turns on the
radio, and we can hear Ted Wilson's

"*Me and My Shadow*." Father Elixir
begins to soft shoe and tap dance to
the delight of Annie and, after a while,
he invites her to join him. and she

does. After some time, you can hear
a knock at the kitchen door which
startles both of them. The priest
goes over and turns down the radio
while Annie yells

ANNIE

Coming! Coming! Wait a minute!

(She signals to the priest to leave
through the back door. He hurriedly
dresses and makes a movement
toward the door, but then turns
around and finishes his drink quickly
and then leaves waving to Annie.
Annie takes the bottle and glasses
and puts them in the cabinet and goes
to the kitchen door and greets Benjy.)

ANNIE

Hi, Benjy. It's always nice to see you... come in... come in.


BENJY

How are you doing, Annie? How's my good luck charm? Today's my day for the ponies, and I need some lucky numbers. Oh, by the way, here's a little something for you.

(Benjy takes a couple of bills and hands them to Annie.)

ANNIE

What's this for, Benjy?

(She puts them on the table beside her.)

BENJY

Last week you gave me the numbers for the trifecta. Keep this up and we'll both be on *Easy Street*.

(The kitchen door opens and Tommy walks in. He's obviously high.)

ANNIE

That would be nice, huh, Benjy? Sit down and

cut the deck.

BENJY

(as he is doing that)

By the way, I saw Mel at the track. He told me
he got bad news about his brother George. You
know he was stationed in France?

ANNIE

I know exactly where he's stationed. My son
Charlie is in his outfit. What did they hear and
when did they hear it?

(Her anguish is evident.)

BENJY

He didn't tell me the details, Annie. But I'm sure you don't have to worry. I mean...


ANNIE

Did he say that George was killed or that he was missing in action?

BENJY

He didn't tell me. He just said he had bad news. Honest, Annie. You're worrying for nothing. You would have heard by now if there was something wrong with Charlie. Just get it out of your mind and help me pick my numbers. I promise you, Annie, if I win again tonight, you won't have to work for a year if you don't want to. There, isn't that something nice to think about? What do, you say, Annie?

ANNIE

It's no good now, Benjy. I can't think straight now... Charlie's filling my mind.

TOMMY

Hey, Benjy baby, how are you doing? Hey, look here, a present for me.

(He bends down and takes the money that's on the table.)

What do you say, Benjy? Why don't you take this up to the track and double it for me, huh?

(He throws it across the table toward Benjy.)

BENJY

Why don't you take it up there yourself? You're spending half your

life up there anyway, and the other
half in every saloon in town.

TOMMY

No, that's where you're wrong,
Benjy. There's a couple I haven't
hit yet. But I will. Just give me
time.


BENJY

Time's about all you've got, war
hero. Too bad they didn't give
medals for the kind of thing you were
doing in the service. You could
pawn those and be rich instead of
taking money from your old lady.


TOMMY

(goes running across the
room and grabs Benjy by
the collar)

Why you little son of a bitch! I should

kick your face in.

BENJY

Why don't you, Tommy? Why don't
you? Punching 60-year-old men and
taking the last dollar from your
widowed mother... that's the sort of
thing that's perfect for you, isn't it? Go
ahead, hit me.

ANNIE

(She gets up from the table
and separates. the two of
them.)

Stop it! Stop it, you two! I
won't have any of that around
here. Tommy, why don't you
go and lie down. You're tired.

TOMMY

Yeah, I suppose you're right. He not worth
dirtying my hands on.

BENJY

Big talk, Tommy. Big talk. Where was all this
brave guy stuff when your platoon needed you?
Don't try to hide it. I know all about it.

TOMMY

You shut up! You hear me! You shut up!

BENJY

What's the matter? Haven't you told your
mother yet?

ANNIE

Benjy, that's enough. Leave him alone. Don't say

anymore.

BENJY

I don't believe it. I don't believe my ears. You haven't told her! Here you are blowing every penny she can scrape together living like a goddamn king when you really should be rotting away in a prison somewhere.

TOMMY

You're wrong! You're goddamn wrong! They didn't find me guilty. They couldn't prove it.

BENJY

Yeah, well, they proved enough. They were able to kick your ass out of the service; and if it wasn't for your brother Charlie, they would have nailed you but good.

ANNIE

Charlie? What does Charlie have to do with any of this? Tommy, tell me.

TOMMY

It's nothing, Ma. This little bastard is lying.
The only thing he knows about are nags and
whores.


BENJY

Yeah, you're right, Tommy, I'm an
expert on both those things. Especially
whores. And you're one of the biggest I've
ever met.

(Tommy picks up the deck of cards
and flings them at Benjy.)


TOMMY

Get out of here! Get out of here! Get the fuck
out of my house!

ANNIE

Please, Benjy. Please leave.

BENJY

I'm going. Yeah, I'm going. But don't let him lie
to you anymore. Don't let him fool you,
Annie. Remember, you can spread shit so thin
sometimes you can hardly see it. But if you get
up close to it, the smell gives it away.

TOMMY

You should know. You've had your nose in it enough.

ANNIE

I want both of you to stop right now.

BENJY

I'm on my way, Annie. But before I go I want to congratulate you on your new daughter-in-law. I haven't met her yet; but if I know Charlie, I'm sure she's a beauty. So long, Annie.

(He leaves
the kitchen.)


TOMMY

(Goes to the cabinet, pulls out the bottle of liquor, and fills up a glass and puts them both on the table in front of him)

> She's a beauty, all right. He had to
> be half in the bag when he married
> her.

ANNIE

You're wrong to say that! She hasn't
been here long... we don't even know
her, yet.

TOMMY

If she's here any longer, every guy
in town is going to get to know her.

ANNIE

Stop that! You're talking about your
brother's wife. It's just that she's
from another country, and her
customs are different.

TOMMY

The only thing different about her
customs is that she's used to getting

paid for them in francs. And probably not too many of those. I don't
know what a quarter is worth over
there.

### ANNIE

Will you stop that kind of talk if I tell
you she's pregnant...that she's
carrying Charlie's baby?

### TOMMY

What?

### ANNIE

Yes, she told me last night.

### TOMMY

My kid brother's always been a sap.
But this takes the cake. How the
hell did she ever convince him that
that was his kid.

ANNIE

Of course, it is! Why else would he marry
her? He loves her, and he wants her to have
the baby here. And so that's what I want. So,
no more remarks, okay?

TOMMY

Sure, Mum, sure. Whatever you say. Just
don't be surprised if that kid comes out looking
like half of General Patton's brigade.

> (The bedroom door opens, and
> Simone enters, a French tart in all
> respects. She's just awoken
>
> so, her makeup is smudged around the
> eyes, her hair disheveled and her
> nightgown frilly and revealing an
> abundant cleavage.)

SIMONE

Bon jour, Mama!

(She walks over and kisses Annie on the cheek, and then turns toward Tommy.)

And how are you today, Tommy?

(She leans over to kiss him, but he moves his head away. She looks down at the glass, picks it up, sniffs it, takes a little sip, puts it down.)

I see you're starting early today.


TOMMY

No, I'm just stopping later than usual. Care to join me? Or are you being careful these days?

SIMONE

What do you mean?

TOMMY

I mean the baby. You haven't forgotten the baby, have you? No one could expect you to remember exactly how he got there. That would be a challenge even for Einstein.

ANNIE

Tommy, you promised.

SIMONE

It's okay, Mama. In France we have the saying that when someone says bad things about you, pay more attention to who said it than what they say.

TOMMY

I know a couple of French sayings, too. You want to hear them, Simone?

SIMONE

Sure, sure, Tommy. I'll make you a deal. I'll hear everything you want to tell me but it's necessary afterwards you listen to me, eh?

TOMMY

What the hell have you got to say to me?


SIMONE .

I have much to say but first I think it would be
better if Mama leaves the room.



TOMMY

That up to her.

ANNIE

(She brings a cup of coffee and places it
in front of Simone. Then she starts
removing her apron.)

I have to go shopping anyway. We are running
out of a few

things.

> (Tommy looks at the bottle of liquor to
> make sure she includes that on her
> shopping list.)

Then, I'm going to visit Mrs. Coury.

> (She takes her coat that's hanging
> on the wall and leaves the kitchen.)

> (After Annie leaves the kitchen,
> Simone goes over to the sink, empties
> the cup of coffee, brings the cup with
> her to the table, takes the bottle of
> liquor and fills the cup.)

TOMMY

Aren't you worried about the kid?

SIMONE

Worried about what? That he'll come out
an alcoholic like his uncle?

TOMMY

Me, his uncle? Don't try to sell me that shit,
Simone. Charlie told me where he met you. It
was an address every GI in Paris knew.

SIMONE

Not every GI, eh, Tommy? There were some who weren't interested in that sort of thing.

(Tommy looks down at his glass and takes a slug.)

But, anyway, you're right. That's where he met me after standing in line behind a lot of lonely frightened boys. And that's where we fell in love. Yes, me, the little whore from Pigalle, Tommy. He fell in love with me. And I left that famous address because I loved him, too. This baby is Charlie's!

TOMMY

What if it is? Why did you have to
marry him?


SIMONE

You know how Charlie is. He wouldn't have it any other way. But I'm no fool, Tommy. I know I can 't run away from my past. Who knows that better than you? I'm only going to stay here long enough to have the baby, and then I'm going back to France.

TOMMY

You mean you're going to leave the
baby here?

SIMONE

Yes, I know Charles will find somebody better for him and the baby.

TOMMY

I don't see how you could do something like that. How can you sit there and talk so easy about leaving your baby?

with somebody else?


SIMONE

Easy??!!

(She starts laughing.)

Easy!!! If I wanted the easy way out of anything, you'd be the first person I'd ask. This is the most difficult thing for any woman, but what choice do I have? If I stayed here with my baby, I'd be afraid all the time that someone like you would try to poison his mind against me or keep reminding Charlie that I was no good for him. No, Tommy, I'm not like you. Charlie has given me the chance to do one good thing with my life, and I'm not going to run away from it.

(She starts to sob a little and then catches herself, wipes her tears with her hands, and picks up the coffee cup and takes a sip and then pushes it away.)

Now, I'm going to give you another chance, Tommy.

TOMMY

What do you mean?

SIMONE

Nobody else knows about my plan. I'm going to need some help.

TOMMY

Why should I help you?

SIMONE

Not me, Tommy. You owe me nothing, but Charlie... you owe him what's left of your life.

TOMMY

I have to think about it.

SIMONE

You have to do something about it, not think about it. You've got to climb out of this sewer you're digging for yourself.

TOMMY

For what?

SIMONE

For your mother, for your sister, for your
brother. For Christ's sake, stop thinking about
yourself. Don't you see? This is your chance
for doing something good, too. Your chance to
start wiping away the nightmare that must haunt
you. That's why you get such little sleep, I know.
Because when you close your eyes, everything
comes back, doesn't it?

TOMMY

Oh, God! Does it come back! It comes
back in technicolor. Even the smells, even
the screams!

(He picks up the glass and he
looks at it.) This stuff doesn't touch it
anymore.


SIMONE

What about the other stuff, Tommy?


TOMMY


What are you talking about?

SIMONE

What am I talking about? You think I saw
all those guys over there without learning
something?

>(She leans over and pushes up his
>sleeve.)

There aren't mosquito bites. God, Tommy!
Do something while you can.


TOMMY

Maybe it's too late.

>(Just then we hear a loud explosion-type
>sound and Tommy dives under the table)


SIMONE

It's only a car backfiring outside,
Tommy... come out... there's nothing
to be afraid of.

(Tommy gets back onto the kitchen chair, fingers his hair back into place and takes a slug of his drink)

TOMMY

I told you it was too late.

SIMONE

It's not too late! You haven't been able to stop those nightmares with the alcohol and the drugs, have you? Answer me, have you?

(Tommy just keeps staring at the table.)

Then try something else. Try doing something good for someone who loves you. Haven't you ever done anything good in your life?

TOMMY

Where do you get off asking me if I've
ever done anything good in my life?
What do you think they gave me those
ribbons for? Sitting in my foxhole,
playing with myself?

SIMONE

Or maybe playing with somebody else? Eh,
Tommy? But, no, they couldn't make enough
ribbons for that.

TOMMY

Why you little slut! If you weren't pregnant,
I'd belt you for that.


SIMONE

And I'd deserve it. You see how easy it is to
use someone's weakness to hurt them? How
about a truce, what do you say? We both
could use someone now. We both have
screams to silence.... tell me when yours
started.

TOMMY

Way back... When the commanding
officer first told us, we were going
to Iwo Jima. I couldn't even
pronounce it. The name sounded like
hee-bee-gee-bees to me, but now I
know that's because I was listening to
the sounds my scared gut was making.


SIMONE

Do you ever talk to anyone about

how frightened  were?


TOMMY


I never want to talk about it; but
every once in a while, I get this
feeling like I'm going to choke if I
don't get it out. And then I get

angry, so angry that I have to
punch my fists against a wall to
keep from screaming my head
off...You can only stomach so much
hatred and fear.

There's a definite limit. It's different
for each person, but you know
you've reached it because it spills
over and stains everyone around
you, so you become frightened of
getting too close to anyone.

SIMONE

You mean you become afraid
of getting too close to anyone
new, but you can't stain
anyone whose known and
loved you all your life...like the
people around you here. The
fabric's too tightly woven.
Maybe you can soil them, but
you can't stain them... It was the
killing...that's what bothered

you most, wasn't it,
Tommy...The killing.

TOMMY

That wasn't the worst part. The
worst part was seeing

the ones you didn't kill--the ones that
were almost killed and their loved
ones who wish you had killed them,
too. It's their faces that I see at
night. It's their wailing that wakes
me up on my sweat-soaked sheets ...
then you remember your buddies--
the ones who went through boot
camp with you, the ones who were
always around when you needed
them. But it's the ones that you let
down that really get to you.    That's
the worst, that's the bottom of the
sewer
you were talking about. You can't
hurt any more than that.

SIMONE

Charlie says he never believed you
did it intentionally. Things were
happening too fast...you couldn't do
anything more than you did. And he
said your mind was all screwed up
from the junk you were taking... so it
really wasn't your fault.

TOMMY

If only I could believe that! Sweet Jesus, I wish
I could believe that.

SIMONE

Charlie thinks the world of you. He's your kid
brother and he loves you and now, after what
happened to him, he's going to need you more
than ever. So, will I.

TOMMY

What do you mean? What happened to him?

SIMONE

Charlie was in a land mine explosion and the shrapnel got into both his eyes and he's blind.

TOMMY

Oh, my god!! My mother's going to go crazy!

SIMONE

Charlie knows that and that's why he made me promise not to tell anyone till gets rehabilitated. They are teaching him braille and have given him a seeing eye dog those will help him get through the physical disability but he's going to need much more to get through the emotional disability, and that's where you come in. He's going to have to rely on you to help your mother and sister accept this and I am going to have to rely on you to help him raise his child especially of it's a boy. You're going to have to get strong for all of us and I am here to help you as much as I can.

It's going to take time and a lot talking. It's going to take a lot of tears, Tommy. Only tears can wash away that kind of guilt. Don't bury those people inside you. Bury them out there. And cry over those graves. That kind of mourning can help you. It'll give you enough time to work things out, you'll see. Be patient...Don't try and do it all at once. Take it almost to the breaking point each time, and you'll be able to push that breaking point further and further away... Right now, I think we're reaching one of those breaking points. Anyway, I know I am. What do you say? Are you going to help us? Charlie said I could rely on you.

TOMMY

Is that what he told you? Then, at least we have one thing in common, Simone.


SIMONE

What's that?

TOMMY

My kid brother never could pick a winner.

ACT III

SETTING; A confessional. Father Elixir is
seated in the center reading and we see him
occasionally feign a slight cough and take a
small flask from somewhere inside his cassock
and have a swallow. His whole appearance is
still slightly disheveled. Joey comes in next
and enters the right side of the confessional.
Richie enters the left and immediately takes
out his magazine and starts thumbing through
it. But he soon starts moving around because

he has to go to the bathroom.

FATHER ELIXIR

(sliding open the portal on Joey's side)

Bless you. May God give you the grace to make a good confession.

JOEY

Bless me, Father, for I have sinned. It has been one week since my last confession, and these are my sins. First of all, I did all the same things I did the week before, but that's not really why I'm here today.

FATHER ELIXIR

Wait a minute. Not so fast. What do you mean all the "*same things*" as last week?

JOEY

What's the matter? Don't you remember? They're always the same. You know...having dirty thoughts and touching myself and stealing penny candy from the drug store and...

## FATHER ELIXIR

Hold on, hold on... how many times... you've got to tell me how many times you did these things.

## JOEY

Which things? Stealing penny candy... not too many... maybe only about three or four...because Pop McKelliget is seeing much better since he got those new bifocal glasses.

## FATHER ELIXIR

What about the other things?

> (Meanwhile we can see Richie
> squirming around more and more
> on his side of the confessional. He
> lifts his hand to knock at his portal but
> hesitates.)

JOEY

Oh, you mean having dirty thoughts and touching myself? Well, they sort of go hand in hand... if you pardon the expression.

(Richie by now is beside himself...he has to go to the bathroom very badly, so he decides to rap on the portal.)

FATHER ELIXIR

(obviously surprised by the rapping, speaks to Joey)

You'll have to wait a minute, my son, some poor soul is obviously pained by the remorse swelling inside him. You continue to search your conscience while he relieves himself of his burden.

(He closes Joey's portal and opens

Richie's.)

RICHIE

Thank God, you finally made it

FATHER ELIXIR

Isn't it wonderful to know that the pressure will
soon be off your immortal soul?

RICHIE

That's not exactly where I'm feeling the
pressure right now, Father.

FATHER ELIXIR

Let us begin... may Almighty God give you
the grace to make a good confession.

RICHIE

Right now, I hope He gives me a little longer
control over my bladder.

## FATHER ELIXIR

What did you say?


## RICHIE

Nothing, nothing... let's hurry up... Bless me, Father for I have sinned. It has been one week since my last confession and these are my sins. I had dirty thoughts about sixty times... more or less...

## FATHER ELIXIR

How long did you say it had been since your last confession?


## RICHIE

One week... Joey and me come every week because our folks give us a quarter to go to the movies.

## FATHER ELIXIR

Well, we can discuss that part later... but you mean to tell

me that you've only been away from the confessional one week, and you had dirty thoughts, as you call them,
sixty times?

## RICHIE

All right, all right... don't get too excited... maybe more like seventy but, honest, it couldn't be much more than that. Please let's hurry, unless this place is waterproof.

## FATHER ELIXIR

Seventy... seventy! You mustn't think about

anything else!

RICHIE

Now you sound like Joey. I'm sure if you saw
this magazine, you'd have dirty thoughts, too...
anybody

would... well, maybe not priests... they put stuff
in your food or something, don't they?

FATHER ELIXIR

What magazine are you talking about? It
must be a piece of the devil's work!

RICHIE

(really feeling Mother Nature's call)

Look, Father, I haven't got time to tell you all
about the magazine. I'll leave it with you for a
little while and I'll be back...I can't stand it
any longer. I have to leave.

FATHER ELIXIR

Don't do that... open your heart to the Holy
Spirit. He'll show you what you must do.

RICHIE

Believe me, I know what I must do! He's
welcome to come along but He'd have to
be a fast runner.

JOEY

(He starts knocking on his portal.)

Father, I know that's Richie you're talking to,
open up, open up!

FATHER ELIXIR

What is going on here? I can't hear both your
confessions at once.

RICHIE

Oh, it's only Joey. It's okay. Open his
side... he must want to tell me
something.

FATHER ELIXIR

Tell you something! He's supposed to be
talking to no

one but me in here! Oh, and God, of course

(He raises his eyes heavenward, apologetically.).

(Impatiently, Joey slides back the door himself and starts talking past a very ruffled Father Elixir.)

JOEY

Richie, why are you hogging in on my turn? We agreed that I'd go first, because I never have as much to tell him as you do and that way I can go back and get the quarters.

RICHIE

I know, but I didn't plan on this...I mean I gotta go... I gotta go so bad, my ears are beginning to leak!!

FATHER ELIXIR

Boy, boys! This is highly irregular! I can only hear one confession at a time. If the Monsignor ever walks by and sees this, he'll

have me sent off somewhere to dust cata-
combs or worse still, preside over every
meeting of the Ladies' Auxiliary!!


JOEY

Is the Monsignor really as strict as they say?


FATHER ELIXIR

Strict!? Let me tell you, he wants that rectory
so quiet that the only person he would hire as
a housekeeper was a deaf mute! Get closer.
Wait until you hear this!

> (We see Richie's and Joey's faces
> pressing through their portals and,
> suddenly, looking from side to side at
> the close proximity of the boys, brings
> Father Elixir to his senses.)

What the hell am I doing? Now both of you
get back where you belong.

(He pushes both heads back into
their respective cubicles and slides
the doors.)

I can only handle one of you at a time, and
I'm not even sure I can do that anymore.
Please, it's getting late

(and then half mumbling to himself and

blessing himself)

God, give me strength.

(He pulls out his flask, takes a quick
slug, hears the knocking from Richie's
side, puts his flask quickly away and
opens Richie's portal.)

RICHIE

Look, Father, like I told you before, I've got an
easy way to handle this...I'm going to leave the
*"piece of the devil's work"* with you. You figure
out how much penance I owe, and tell Joey, and
him and me can do our penance together during
the movies' intermission! *See* how easy? Now

I really have to go or else you're going to have
to look for a pair of water wings.

> (He runs out of his side of the
> confessional, throws open Father
> Elixir's door, drops the magazine
> in his lap, slams the door shut, and
> makes a B-line out of the church.)


FATHER ELIXIR

> (He reaches down, picks up the
> magazine, just

puts it on his lap without looking
at it, closes the portal on Richie's
side and opens the portal on
Joey's side.)

Now, my son, I hope the hand of God has

reached you.

JOEY

From the knocking on the walls and the
door slamming, I've been hearing around
this place, he's been trying to reach
someone, Father.

FATHER ELIXIR

What you heard were the cries of help from
a tormented soul. A soul that had been
lured into performing immoral acts
through the literature of the devil.

> (With that he taps the magazine and
> looks
>
> down at it. He is obviously
> intrigued by the cover and very
> cautiously peeks at the contents with
> obviously growing interest.)

JOEY

Father, Father, are you there? Let me tell you
the real reason why I'm here so I can go and
meet Richie.

FATHER ELIXIR

(His perusal of the magazine is
interrupted by Joey's question, so he
closes it, keeping his thumb
between the pages, keeping his
place.)

Oh, yes, my son. Of course. What is it that's
troubling you?

JOEY

Well, I think what Richie and I did with Marcia
the other night was bad. I'm not sure how
bad; but it was the first time I did anything
like that, and my conscience has been
bothering me.

FATHER ELIXIR

Who's Marcia? And what did you do?

JOEY

Oh, Marcia's a girl our age; but she's really
built, Father. You probably don't know what
I mean by "*really built*".

FATHER ELIXIR

(He opened the magazine to a
fascinating page...in fact, he takes
his glasses off and wipes them, and
puts them back on.)

I think I have a pretty good picture of what you
mean, my son.

(Father Elixir turns the page and is
obviously astounded by what he
sees this time to the extent that he
takes a handkerchief from his
pocket and wipes his brow.)

What sort of things did you do with Marcia?

JOEY

Well, we tried to lay on top of her and feel her.

FATHER ELIXIR

All over? You felt her all over?

JOEY

Well, just about.

FATHER ELIXIR

That's nice. That's very nice.

(as he keeps slowly turning the page).

JOEY

What did you say, Father?

FATHER ELIXIR

I'm just praying to myself here. Go on, what else did you do?

JOEY

Well, we didn't do much more than that.

But she did.

FATHER ELIXIR

She did?

(Pointing to the page in front of him)

Did she do any of this?

JOEY

Any of what?

FATHER ELIXIR

(still pointing to the page)

This oral, I mean, immoral stuff?

JOEY

How did you know?

FATHER ELIXIR

How did I know about what?

JOEY

That there was oral stuff?

FATHER ELIXIR

Oh, I don't know. It must have been divine inspiration. What I want to know is did you enjoy that immoral act?

JOEY

Well, to tell you the truth, I got away before she did much to

me. But poor Richie!

FATHER ELIXIR

What do you mean, *'poor Richie'*?

JOEY

Well, after a while, I think, she started hurting him with her teeth...she wears braces.

FATHER ELIXIR

Jesus, Mary and Joseph!

JOEY

Still praying to yourself in there, Father?

FATHER ELIXIR

Playing with myself? You impudent young man!

JOEY

Praying, Father, praying. I asked you if you were praying to yourself. Is there something wrong with you today, Father? You're acting different...are my sins that bad?

FATHER ELIXIR

No, it's my sins.

JOEY

Your sins? What kind of *sins* could you have? I bet you never have to go to confession.

FATHER ELIXIR

Oh, yes, I do; and I'm going to have to go pretty soon.

JOEY

You're so close to God that I bet that if you were doing something wrong, he'd perform some

miracle to let you know how upset
He was.


FATHER ELIXIR

A miracle? Wasted on me? I'd have
to be doing something very terrible.

JOEY

That's what I meant! You're too
hard on yourself. After all, you're
human like everybody else. That's
how I look at it anyway.

FATHER ELIXIR

Oh, yes, I'm human all right. And
I'm reminded of it very explicitly at
times. But you are right about
certain feelings being universal but
giving into them is where the line has
to be drawn.

JOEY

Well, maybe if you give into them all
the way, it's wrong. But a little
pleasure isn't going to hurt anyone.
My grand-mother says: God taught us
to laugh as well as to cry.

FATHER ELIXIR

Your grandmother's right and

(He starts opening the book
again slowly.)

maybe a little enjoyment isn't so bad after all.

(Just as he opens the page, the picture of St. Jude falls out. He bends over and picks it up.)

Oh, my God! St. Jude falling out of this magazine! That's the miracle we were talking about.

(He raises his eyes to heaven.)

Boy, are you upset with me? I've really done it this time, haven't I?

JOEY

Father, I don't know what's going on in there, but could you possibly calm down long enough just to give me penance? I want to get to the movies. This is the last episode of "*The Perils of Pauline.*"

(He hears Father Elixir exiting the confessional. So, Joey opens his door and starts speaking excitedly.)

Where are you going in such a hurry, Father?

FATHER ELIXIR

To Rome, my son, to Rome...I hope it's not too late!

(He exits off stage.)

JOEY

Hey, Father. Wait a minute. You dropped your magazine. (Joey picks up the magazine.)

Geez, I wonder how many of these Richie's cousin brought back from France.

(He opens the magazine.)

Wow, here's a page I never saw before. Look at all those positions.

(As he's talking, he backs into the priest's section of the confessional and sits down and starts perusing the page.)

(As we look at the confessional with Joey sitting in the middle with his magazine, we see the sisters Bella and Delia walking onto the stage. Delia goes into the left section of the confessional first, and then Bella goes into the right.

Joey is so intrigued by the magazine that he is unaware the sisters have entered until he hears a knocking from Delia's side of the confessional.)

JOEY

Jesus Christ!

DELIA

I hear you praying in there, Father. I'm back again to tell you all about all the naughty things I did this week. I was ahead of Bella so open my side first. Oh, I know you're going to be so angry with me when you hear what I've got to tell you. I hope you won't punish me too much. But whatever it is, I deserve it. I know I deserve it.

(We can see Bella on her side of the confessional pressing her ear as close as possible to the portal trying to hear her sister's confession. Joey, in the meantime, is showing obvious

179

bewilderment with his predicament; but Delia's wrapping on the portal forces him to slide it open.)


JOEY

Ah, ah, what can I do for you?


DELIA


Father, you never, started off my confession like that before. I told you I've been bad, but at least aren't you going to offer me God's help?

JOEY

Oh, yes, of course. May God help you and me to make a good confession.

## DELIA

Well, as you know it has been one week
since my last confession; but what a week
it's been, let me tell you! I went to a
fortune teller. Now I know that's a sin by
itself but wait till you hear what she told
me.

> (Bella now is beside herself not
> being able to hear Delia clearly,
> so she reaches in her purse and
> pulls out one of those old-
> fashioned hearing aid horns and
> presses one end of it against the
> portal and the other against her
> ear.)

She said there is a very tall, dark,
handsome man who just can't live without
me and unless I give into him, he is going to
die of a broken heart. Just die. So, you
know what I did, Father?

> (Joey is so petrified of being
> discovered he's afraid to say

anything, but we can see him
shaking his head "*no*,"
emphatically "*no*."


DELIA

Well, I'll tell you. After all, that's what I'm
here for, isn't it? I let the fortune teller put
him right on top of me.

BELLA

(hearing this drops her hearing
device and unwittingly shouts)

No, it wasn't like that at all.

(Joey just about jumps out of his skin
when he hears Bella's voice from the
other side.)

JOEY

It wasn't?

BELLA

No, it wasn't. Open this door, and I'll
tell you just what happened.

(Joey slides her side the

door.)

BELLA

She didn't put anybody on Delia except the
jack and the king.

JOEY

Both of them? She put them

both on her?

DELIA

Is that Bella's voice I hear in there, Father?
Bella, why can't you wait your turn? This
is my confession.

BELLA

Well, don't lie about your sins.

DELIA

I'm telling him just what I feel in my soul. Now

where was I, Father?

JOEY

You were underneath jack and king.

DELIA

Oh, yes, there I was giving myself to the man I
love.

BELLA

You were giving nothing to anyone just like you always do.


DELIA

What do you mean by that remark?

BELLA

You know what I mean.

> (As the two women are arguing, Joey slowly sneaks out of the confessional, opens his arms upwards to heaven as if to say to God: *You take it from here.* As he starts walking off stage, we can still hear Delia and Bella shouting across to one another.)

DELIA

If you mean, I'm saving myself for the man who really worthy of me, you're right.

BELLA

The man's who's really worthy of you has got to be sitting in some mental institution somewhere.

(As the scene fades, we can hear Delia's voice trailing off and Joey waving goodbye to the audience)

SCENE II

SETTING; Kitchen in Annie's tenement. Joey and Annie are seated at the kitchen table.

(Throughout this scene, Joey coughs sporadically. He has a bruise on his face.)

ANNIE

How was the movie?

JOEY

Great. This episode had me on the edge of my seat.

ANNIE

(pointing to the bruise)

Looks like you fell off...

JOEY

This? It's nothing...I just... bumped my head... that's all

ANNIE

I know what will fix it in a hurry... I just baked some of your favorite cookies.

(She gets up to get the cookies.)

JOEY

Not right now...I want to ask you something first.

ANNIE

It must be important...

(She sits back down again.)

JOEY

How come so many people come to visit you every day?

ANNIE

So that's it, is it?... Well, they come to hear about what's in their minds.

JOEY

Why do they need you to tell them what's in their own minds?

ANNIE

Because most people are too busy trying to figure out what other people are thinking and fill their ears with someone else's ideas, so they don't trust their own...they're not used to them. That where I come in.

JOEY

What do you do?

ANNIE

I just listen to what they're telling me about themselves, and I watch their actions. When I'm through, I sort of repeat it all back to them. I act like a mirror, and they think I have magic powers. That's all there is to it. Now why the great interest suddenly?

JOEY

Well, some of the kids have been talking about what you do, and I didn't like what they were saying.

ANNIE

Oh?

JOEY

They were saying you were kind of different from other people. Like, you had some kind of strange power...like a... oh, I don't know.... Grandma.

ANNIE

How about like a witch? Is that what the other kids were saying? Is that why the bruise?

JOEY

(looking down at the table...embarrassed)

Yeah, well sort of... but I know you ain't no witch, Grandma! I told them. Richie and me let some of them have it. They won't be calling you any more names, I promise.

ANNIE

Oh, Joey, Joey. You know why they say that? Because probably one of the parents of each of those kids has been in to see me over the years, and they didn't like what they heard, or they went didn't take the advice I gave them, and things went wrong... and they blame me for it. It's easier to do that than live with the guilt. Can you understand that, love?

JOEY

Kind of...Grandma, but I'm not that sure...I guess I'm stupid.

ANNIE

No, Joey, I'm the stupid one ...

Let me try to explain it in another way. Let's suppose you came to me for help in deciding... if you should become a doctor, for instance.

JOEY

There you go with the doctor business again, Grandma. You know what Dad said about that when I asked him?

ANNIE

No, what?

JOEY

He said that they'd have to start giving the medical school courses over the radio. He said that they'd have, to squeeze them in during the commercial breaks of "*The Lone Ranger*" *show, "Inner Sanctum," and "Henry Aldrich."*

(Annie starts laughing.)

He said, that way maybe I could get a diploma if I sent four box tops and 25 cents! But all kidding aside grandma, do you really think I can become a doctor?

ANNIE

Of course, but I was just using that as an example...I don't know why it's the first thing that came into my head... Honest

(She winks at him.).

Let's go on... So, you come in, sit down, and have a cup of coffee, and we talk... Right off the bat, I can see that you're not only a brilliant conversationalist, but you're also very sensitive and, as a bonus you're...drop dead handsome!

JOEY

So, I take after my grandmother, can I help it? Go on... I'm beginning to like this.

(They're both obviously enjoying this.)

ANNIE

Then I ask if you want me to read the coffee, the cards, or your palm.
What's the difference?
ANNIE
The price... the palm reading's the most expensive.

JOEY

Then, I'll take that.

ANNIE

Okay, sport, give me your hand.

JOEY

Which one?

ANNIE

Are you right handed or left handed?

JOEY

Right handed. But what if I was ambidextrous...like Richie's cousin Ernie?

ANNIE

I guess I'll have to charge twice as much...now give me have your right hand.

> (Joey before extending his hand, opens it, scrutinizes it, rubs it on his trouser pants and then hands it to her sort of apologetically for it not being as clean as it should be. Annie looks at it and gives him a halfhearted reproachful look and continues to talk.)

Very interesting. Very unusual.

JOEY

Unusual? What do you mean? You don't see
any hair growing there, do you?

ANNIE

Hair? No. A little licorice, a little bubble gum,
maybe, but no hair. Why do you ask that?

JOEY

Oh, it nothing. Just another lie I heard from
some of

the kids. Why did you say my hand was
unusual?

ANNIE

Well, you see this line here?

JOEY

Yeah.

ANNIE

Well, that's your interest line. And you see
how it sort of makes a sharp angle here?
That's the unusual thing. Usually, the line
curves.

JOEY

I'll bet you'd see some interesting curves in
Richie's interest line.

ANNIE

What do you mean?

JOEY

Oh, nothing. I was just talking to myself.
So, what about the sharp angle you see?
What does it mean?

ANNIE

Well, it looks like a book.

JOEY

You see a book, a whole book in there,
Grandma? You're sure it not a magazine? Do
you see any French writing?

ANNIE

No, no. The line is too thick for a
magazine. It's definitely a book.

JOEY

Well, that good. For a minute there, I wasn't
sure if I

wanted you to go on with this whole
thing. So, I'm interested in books,
Grandma?

ANNIE

Well, that what I'm seeing here. How did you do in

school last year? Did you pass anything?

(They both start laughing.)


JOEY

Of course, I did, Grandma. I passed everything.

ANNIE

Did you have to work very hard?

JOEY

Really, I didn't spend much time studying except for the new course.


ANNIE

What was that?

## JOEY

General science. Come to think of it that was the largest book I had. It had chapters on a lot of different things. Chemistry and plants and animals and even the human body. Richie and I have spent a lot of time looking at the outside of the human body, but I found out that the inside is just as interesting. Do you know you have over twenty feet of intestine in your stomach? Imagine that? Twenty feet! That would go almost around this kitchen. And if they put all your blood vessels together end to end, I forget how many times around the world it would go. And the human brain, Grandma, has millions and billions of cells and nobody has discovered what most of them do. Can you imagine how exciting it must be for someone to try and discover what some of those cells do? It would be like putting together a giant jigsaw puzzle.

ANNIE

Yes, it would, but even more important because all the work you put into it could pay off by helping people that have something wrong with their brain or even parts of their body that are controlled by certain parts of the brain.

JOEY

Wow! You think you could make some people walk again?

ANNIE

I don't see why not.

JOEY

Wouldn't they be happy? I can't think of anything worse than being crippled, can you, Grandma?

ANNIE

Yes, I can think of a few things. But being crippled is terrible. Any kind of cripple is terrible.

JOEY

What other kind of cripple are you talking

about, Grandma?

ANNIE

Mentally cripple, Joey, mentally cripple. There are all degrees of that, sweetheart: some people can't think straight at all and some are just confused.

JOEY

Those kids that called you a witch were mentally crippled, Grandma. And if they do it again, they're going to be another kind of cripple, I can promise you that.


ANNIE


No, Joey, that's no answer. Those kids are not mentally crippled. They've been told lies by mentally crippled people, and the only way to stop them is not by hitting them with your fists. You hit them with the truth, Joey.


JOEY

Do you always tell the truth, Grandma?

ANNIE

(She smiles.)

That's a good question, Joey. You know I'm beginning to think maybe a lawyer. You'd be a pretty good lawyer. Do I always tell the truth? Well, let's put it this way. I always try to get to the truth in the end but sometimes, I decide it's safer to take a couple of detours on the way.

JOEY

Detours? What kind of detours? Why would
                  you do that?

ANNIE

Sometimes the short route is too dangerous.
For example, the mother or father of one of
your friends comes to see me because they're
having trouble sleeping or stomach trouble,
and I suspect by talking to them that they're
doing something they're feeling guilty about.
Maybe drinking too much or cheating on their
wife or husband. Now I know if I tell them
what I suspect the first time I see them or in
some cases even the first few times, they're
going to deny it because they're coming to me
for something that seems to have no connection
with that

JOEY

You mean screwing around with someone else's
wife can give you agita?

ANNIE

Sometimes, honey, sometimes.


JOEY

I could see, maybe, it if they were fooling around
with Mrs. Kowalski.

(They both start to laugh.)

I bet you have to take some pretty wild
detours sometimes. eh, Grandma?

ANNIE

(laughing)

You're not kidding. Many times, the trips are much longer that I planned and sometimes. I never get to where I wanted to go. I suppose, that's when they start calling me names in front of their kids.

JOEY

Those kids! Whoever is having an affair with any of *their* parents has to be really hard up!

ANNIE

Now wait a minute, Joey. I never said any such thing... Don't walk out of this room with that idea. I was only giving you an example. Remember that.

JOEY

Don't worry. I was only kidding. Come on, what else do you see in my hand?

ANNIE

Well, it takes a long time to become a
doctor...let's look at the lifeline. There it is,
*see?*

JOEY

You mean this one?

ANNIE

Yes.

JOEY

Well, how does it look, Grandma?

ANNIE

It's fine. It's a good long line. The only thing
that is interrupting it is that dry piece of
bubble gum.

(They laugh again.)

JOEY

You're telling the truth, ain't you... You're not taking one of those detours?

ANNIE

Of course, not...

Why do you ask such a foolish thing?

JOEY

Well, I had a real bad coughing spell last night.

ANNIE

Don't worry about it... believe me. No detours necessary.

JOEY

Okay, Grandma, now it's my turn.

I'm going to read your fortune.

Come on give me your hand. I don't care which one.

(Annie starts laughing, and she
gives him her hand.)

JOEY

(scrutinizing her palm)

Um-m. I don't see it. I've got to look more
carefully. It's got to be there.

ANNIE

What don't you see,

sweetheart?

JOEY

Never mind. I'll find it. Here let me move it

over to the light. There it is! The cookie line.

(Annie starts laughing.)

I found it. I can see the cookies you
baked this morning and the line is

pointing to the jar over the refrigerator. And it says that if I don't eat at least a dozen of them, I'm going to have stomach trouble, and I won't be able to sleep

(They both start laughing.)

## SCENE III

SETTING; Nellie's kitchen.

### TED

Did you hear that kid last
night...he was coughing his heart
out?

### NELLIE

> (Holding her head in her
> hands... knowing she
> can't go on deceiving
> herself)

Yes...yes...I heard it...of course, I
heard it! But he was still very tired
from the night of the blackout.
Richie and Marcia were over, and he
didn't get to bed till late... and
besides... there's also some bug that's
going around... even I haven't felt well
the last couple of days.

(She touches her brow
as if to see if she has a
fever.)

TED

Cut it out, Nellie. The boy's sick. The
trouble is you can't face it unless
you're looking into the bottom of a
coffee cup. It's not even right to let
Richie spend so much time with him in
that closed room.

NELLIE

What are you saying? What do you know
about this? You haven't been taking care of
him! You haven't been taking care of either of
us! You and your two damn jobs!

TED

Well, tomorrow I'm not going to those *two
damn jobs*.' I'm taking Joey into Boston. I

won't stand by and watch him die just because you're afraid to face the truth.

NELLIE

You can't do that. They'll take him from me,

forever!

(She bangs the table with her fists

TED

Nellie, Nellie! Listen to me, please... People do come back from those hospitals. Many of them are cured. You can't just think about the ones that didn't make it.

(You can hear Joey coughing loudly next door. Nellie looks up at Ted.)

NELLIE

You promise he'll come back to me. You promise?

TED

I promise.


NELLIE

(She sits at the table with her head
staring down, raising it momentarily
when she, hears the coughing from
Joey's room and then realizing she's
defeated, she speaks)

I can't think anymore, so you'll have to think
for me...you'll have to think for all of us. But
please don't tell him until tomorrow. I don't
want anything to spoil today. Today is going
to be the happiest day ever. Charlie is
expected home this morning. That's what he
said in his letter. I want Joey to enjoy the
homecoming. We've all waited so long.

(She begins to dry her eyes with the
end of her apron and starts pushing
her hair back with her hands.)

I've got to get myself together now and go downstairs and give Mom a hand.

(She goes over to Ted and

squeezes his hand.)

I know you're going to do the

right thing.

(She lays her head against his shoulder.)

It's just so hard for me to see anything right in all of this.

(She pulls her head away and looks at him.)

What you must do is promise me that you won't tell him anything today. I'm not putting it off like I have before. You've got to believe me. It's just that today is so special, and I want him to enjoy being with his uncle again. You will wait, won't you?

TED

I promise.

>   (She leaves. Then Ted goes over to
>   Joey's bedroom door and knocks.)

TED

Joey, Joey! Are you up, son? Can I come in? I've got a

surprise for you.


JOEY

>   (coughing sporadically throughout the
>   rest of the dialogue in this scene)

Sure, Dad. Come in. I was just getting up away. It almost time for my programs.

TED

That's right. In a little while, I'll be hearing
Mrs. Aldrich screaming for Henry. You
really enjoy those programs, don't you?

JOEY

Oh, they're great, Dad. You should
listen to them sometime.

TED'

That's exactly what I plan on doing this
morning. I'm going to spend the whole time
here with you enjoying those shows and blowing
bubbles.

JOEY

Blowing bubbles?

TED

That's my surprise. Close your eyes and open
your hands.

(Joey does as he instructed, and Ted takes out several pieces of bubble gum and places them in each of Joey's hands.)

JOEY

Double bubble! Dad, double bubble! Where did you get it? We haven't been able to buy it for months.

TED

Oh, a friend of mine at work owed me a favor. I was able to get his wife a pair of nylons when I got your mother's.

JOEY

This is great. I'm going to save a piece for Richie. You know he's collected all the cartoons from every piece of bubble gum he's ever had.

TED

Richie's a good friend, isn't he, Joey?

JOEY

He is, Dad. The best. I'm going to miss him.

TED

*'Miss him'?*

JOEY

When we move? When you buy us a
house? Mum said you were working hard
for it. I know you'll do it.

> (He starts coughing and reaches for
> the medicine bottle on the night table
> and takes a slug and gradually the
> coughing subsides.)

TED

That cough is getting tough, huh?

JOEY

Some days are worse than others. Mom says I'm
still tired from the night of the blackout.

TED

Your mother told me Marcia was over here that
night. That may be another reason why you're
tired, eh?

JOEY

What do you mean? We just sat here and
listened to the radio.

TED

Joey, I've seen Marcia.

JOEY

(a little embarrassed)

Well, she is growing up...some places more
than others. But it really doesn't bother me too
much.

### TED

Oh, no? Well, I remember when I was your age, and it used to bother me a lot. You know this may be a good time to have a little talk about the birds and the bees.

### JOEY

The birds and the bees, Dad? You've got to be kidding. You really want to talk about sex, right?

Well, don't bother because I know everything.

### TED

Where did you learn it from?

### JOEY

Mostly from the big guys. They talk about it after school or when we're hanging around the corner. They don't just talk about the fun things either. They talk about the bad things that can happen to you, too, like if you play with yourself a lot... you can go mental or grow hair on the palms of your hands or even go blind. Dad, do you think that's why Uncle Harry wears such thick glasses?

(They both laugh.)

TED

Joey. don't think you can learn all there is about sex only

from the other guys.

JOEY

Oh, I don't. Richie has this magazine. It shows mostly girls with no clothes on. It doesn't show exactly how to do it, but it does show you where.

TED

Everybody is telling you how to do it and where to do it, but we have to talk about when to do it.

JOEY

Richie and I thought the night of the blackout would have been a pretty good time, but things got a little crazy. See, Marcia said that Richie and I were going about it all the wrong way, and she started to show us the right way. But she got out of control and wouldn't get off of Richie and me.

TED

You mean she was on top of both of you? At the
same time?

JOEY

Yeah. I don't know what parts Richie had, but I
sure can tell you where her knees were.

TED

Oh, my God! You guys didn't...

JOEY

Relax, Dad. We didn't do anything. Marcia
was completely in charge; and if my coughing
hadn't stopped her, no one would ever have to
talk to either Richie or me about sex because
we would have been ruined for life.

TED

Listen, Joey, experimenting with sex can be
a dangerous business.

JOEY

You're telling me! I won't be able to ride my
bike for a week, and poor Richie...he must be
peeing in three different directions at the
same time. Look, Dad, it's almost ten o'clock.
Can't we talk about this some other time?


TED

Sure, Joey, sure. How about a piece of that
bubble gum?

> (Joey takes a piece out of his pocket
> and hands it to his dad. and he opens
> one up for himself. They both read the
> comic strip and start laughing a bit.
> Joey reaches over and turns on the
> radio
>
> and you can hear: *HENRY? HENRY
> ALDRICH?* The scene fades while
> they're both attempting to blow
> bubbles.)

# SCENE IV

SETTING: Annie's kitchen. Annie's at the stove, Tommy's at the table and Nellie is pacing nervously.

TOMMY

Will you sit down. You're driving me crazy... It's tough enough trying to stay away from the booze!

ANNIE

This is the time of day... those damn telegrams come... How can she relax?

TOMMY

But he's coming home today... You've got nothing to worry about.

NELLIE

No... nothing to worry about...

(she smiles at the irony)

nothing at all... Since when did you stop drinking?

TOMMY

(looks at his watch)

Eleven hours, 13 minutes, 8...oops...10 seconds ago...I promised Mom I'd be sober when Charlie arrives...Where's Simone?

ANNIE

She's getting ready. She wants to look lovely

for Charlie.

TOMMY

Lovely, eh? By the time she manages that, his furlough will be over

NELLIE

Lay off her. She's been very nice to you.

TOMMY

Well, why not? I'm a likeable guy especially when I'm sober.

NELLIE

It'd be tough to prove that.

TOMMY

Mom, she's picking on me again.

ANNIE

I'm not even listening to you two...I just want to get this meal done. I want it to be perfect--all his favorites.

TOMMY

I don't remember your fussing that much for me... but maybe that's because I didn't send you a bride with a surprise package inside.

ANNIE

I cooked for three days before you got here, but you wouldn't touch a thing and don't think I didn't worry about your bringing home one of those Japanese *gotcha girls*!

TOMMY

(laughing)

Not "*gotcha girls*," Mum...Geisha girls!

ANNIE

Oh, yeah. Billie told your Aunt Stella all
about them. And from what she told me, I
don't care what you call them to start off... by
the time they're through with you, they've
gotcha alright...by the you know what.

TOMMY

I don't believe you said that, Mum.

NELLIE

I never heard you talk like that before.

ANNIE

That's because I never heard such things
before. And you know your aunt, she
probably only got half the story.

TOMMY

(winking at Nellie)

Mum, now that you mention it, there was
something I wanted to talk to you about. I
didn't know how I was going to bring it up,
but I don't think I'll ever get a better chance.


ANNIE

(She turns from stove
apprehensively.)

What, Tom? What have you got to tell me?
You didn't get involved with one of those
girls over there, did you?


TOMMY

Nothing to worry about, Mum...I mean, only
a few of them got pregnant.

ANNIE

Only a few of them!!

TOMMY

I'm telling you, don't worry...I have no
intention of marrying any of them.

ANNIE

Well, I'm thankful for that, but what's going to happen to them?


TOMMY

Well, you know what a softie I am? I insisted that when the kids were old enough, they send them here for you to take care of. I was mostly worried about the triplets.

ANNIE

Triplets? Oh, my God!!

> (Tommy goes running over to her
> and gives her a big hug.)


TOMMY

Just kidding, Mum... They're only twins.

> (He starts laughing.)

ANNIE

(She picks up the stirring spoon
and starts threatening Tommy
with it.)

If you don't stop teasing me, I'll

(She's interrupted by Simone coming into the
room.).

SIMONE

Charlie?

(She looks around the room.)

Where is he? I just heard him.

NELLIE

He's not here yet, Simone. You heard Tommy.

SIMONE

You sound just like Charlie when you laugh.

Doesn't he?

ANNIE

People used to say that all the time.

SIMONE

I never realized it. That's funny, isn't it? But
you know, that's the first time I can remember
hearing you laugh.

TOMMY

I've been too busy.

ANNIE

Oh, you'll hear him laugh a lot when Charlie
gets home. They're always joking around.
Right, Nellie?

NELLIE

Nobody is safe when those two get together.
Remember the time when Father Elixir came to
bless the house?

TOMMY

Yeah, and Charlie put the crushed
mothballs in the incense? What a stink!

(He starts laughing.)

I don't know who left the house faster... the
devil or Charlie and me.

NELLIE

I think it was Father Elixir. It took Mom and
me a week to air out the house.

ANNIE

I don't know why I'm laughing your father almost
killed you both!

TOMMY

Yeah, and I don't know why. We got rid
of every cockroach in the building for at
least two months!

I'll bet Mr. Kowalski just thought it
was one of his wife's new recipes. In
fact, her kitchen never smelled better.

(they all laugh)
                SIMONE

Charlie never told me that story.


                ANNIE

I'm sure there are a lot of stories he
hasn't told you about him and his
brother. In fact, I wish I never heard
them either.


                SIMONE

They were that bad, huh?



                ANNIE

You wouldn't believe it...The one I
remember best was when the boys
decided to play gas station attendant.
                TOMMY

        Oh, not that one... our asses were raw for
a week for that stunt.
                SIMONE

What happened? I love to hear stories
about when Charlie was a boy.

TOMMY

You don't want to hear this one.

SIMONE

I do... please!

NELLIE

I'll tell you. I was there. Dad was still alive, and he had borrowed Uncle Sammy's new car. The car didn't have ten miles on it. These two clowns got up early and decided the care needed more gasoline... so they filled the tank with sand!

SIMONE

Sand?!!

NELLIE

To the brim... and screwed the cap back on so everything looked fine... Mom packed a big box full of food, and we all got in the car. The boys made me promise not to say a thing. I'll never forget the look on Dad's face when he tried to start the motor.

TOMMY

I'll never forget the look on his face when he found out what happened. Both him and Uncle Sammy had a go at us. Whatever part one missed, the other got. By the time we could sit down again... we had forgotten how to.

NELLIE

Well, they taught you a lesson you
              never forgot. TOMMY

You're telling me... in fact, years later, all the
guys were talking about what we could do for
work. Someone suggested running a gas station
and Charlie and me both stood up!

              (rubbing his behind)

SIMONE

You're going to have such a good time talking
about those days with Charlie.

TOMMY

You're right. I'd almost forgotten how good
they were.

              (Just then there are two rings on the
              doorbell. Nellie looks at the clock
              and walks to the window facing the
              back of the house and just stares
              out, Annie begins nervously
              stirring the food, and Simone looks
              apprehensively at Tommy who tries
              to appear upbeat.)

TOMMY

Hey, all of you. Did you hear that? Charlie's home. My kid brother is back.


ANNIE

I can't leave this now. It'll burn. Nellie you stay here and help me I'm so excited I can't think straight. Tommy,you and Simone go bring him to me...please. Bring him to me...hurry!!

TOMMY

You bet your life I'll hurry. Come on, Simone.

(We hear his voice fading down

the hallway.) Charlie, here I

come...Charlie, it's your big brother...

# CURTAIN

Made in the USA
Middletown, DE
09 October 2023

40316497R00139